HEIRS AND GRACES

HEIRS AND GRACES

GERALD HAMMOND

First published in Great Britain in 2005 by
Allison & Busby Limited
Bon Marché Centre
241-251 Ferndale Road
London SW9 8BJ

http://www.allisonandbusby.com

A catalogue record for this book is available from
the British Library.

10 9 8 7 6 5 4 3 2 1

ISBN 0 7490 8309 3

Printed and bound in Wales by
Creative Print and Design, Ebbw Vale

GERALD HAMMOND is a retired architect and the creator of the mystery series featuring John Cunningham, a dog breeder in Scotland, and Keith Calder, a gunsmith. He also writes under the pseudonyms Arthur Douglas and Dalby Holden.

Any reader familiar with cruise ships may recognise the green man statue as standing on the Pool Deck of the Marco Polo.

I have tried to be geographically correct with the area of Dornoch and Dornoch Firth. (I return to that area for two reasons. One is that I love the area and go back there as often as I can. The other is sheer laziness. Writing dialect is hard work, but around Inverness is spoken the purest English in Britain.)

I have taken liberties, but only with individual buildings. The characters, however, are absolutely fictitious.

Gerald Hammond

Chapter One

All the best stories have happy endings. This one has a happy beginning. God alone knows, at the time of writing, where it will end. Some sort of a resolution seems to have been reached, but no secret is a secret if anyone knows it, anyone at all.

Grace Gillespie rather doubted that there was an afterlife and she was even more doubtful about the existence of a personal God. She had no objection to Faith – indeed, she felt that belief in God, while probably unfounded, should be an influence for good. What she did believe, with a faith equal to that of the most devout, was that much of the world's violence stemmed either from professional football or from one organised religion or another. Most wars and evil deeds had been and still were done in the name of religion. It was evident that football was an eternal force, far too well established ever to fail, but organised religion seemed to be collapsing under its own weight and the onslaught of science. It would therefore have been against her principles to prop it up, even by such a slight support as to be married in church.

This was a great disappointment to her mother. Mrs Gillespie had begun to despair of ever seeing her only daughter married, and especially not in white. Her hopes of a church wedding, in whatever colour, had risen again when Grace, a freelance physiotherapist, had returned to the far north of Scotland and the vicinity of her native Dornoch and had contracted an alliance with her patient, a depute headmaster who had fallen from a roof.

Mrs Gillespie's joy was diminished when Grace stubbornly insisted that marriage by the registrar and in the presence of the minimum of friends and relations would be more appropriate and quite sufficient for her purposes. But if the ceremony were to be less than the Gillespies had aspired to for the celebration of their daughter's coupling along with the prospect of grandchildren, at least the reception would be worthy of the occasion. Mr Gillespie even considered holding it at nearby Skibo Castle, in emulation of at least one of Madonna's marriages, but on enquiry decided that, although he had been paying into an endowment policy against the event ever since the bride's birth thirty-two years earlier, the cost would be quite beyond his comparatively limited means. The Canmore House Hotel, not far from Skibo Castle geographically but somewhat distant in price, was booked instead, catering organised and a band made up from the groom's former pupils was engaged. This, of course, entailed the sending out of invitations, and the event was immediately in the public domain.

Stuart Campbell, the groom, was well known and liked, not least by his former pupils. Grace, although she had pursued her healing profession for years in far-flung parts of Britain and even, occasionally, abroad, was a local girl. Moreover, the drama entailed in Stuart's fall, the revelation that he had in fact been thrown and the arrests and charging of those responsible had lent the pair a special glamour in the general view. Invitations to the reception were met with almost indecently hasty acceptance.

More surprisingly, when the couple and the small family party arrived at the registrar's office it was to find a substantial throng lying in wait and each one quite determined to attend the civil ceremony. But the registrar's office in Dornoch, along with the other representatives of the local authorities, had been squeezed into a late Victorian building, originally a Manse. Along with the registrar and the happy couple, there was barely room for the bride's parents. The narrow but rambling corridor leading to the wedding room was immediately packed with listening guests who declined by sheer inertia to move, thereby disrupting all business in other council departments.

The subsequent orgy of confetti throwing had the caretaker demanding extra special remuneration. Jenny Welles, a friend of the bride and a professional photographer, was so stretched to record the event (partly with sales to the local papers in mind) that she was unable to get inside the entrance door at all.

As a rough rule of thumb, the time required for a group of people to walk a route or complete a task can be calculated by taking the time required by one person for the same activity and multipling it by the square root of the number of people taking part. The distance involved was sufficient to require the use of cars and a hired coach. The limited parking area assigned to the building was by now packed with cars, as were the adjoining streets, and because tradition demanded that the bridal Rolls get away first, much time was lost in what the groom described as a two-dimensional version of Rubik's cube.

The wedding party arrived at the Canmore House Hotel rather after the appointed time. Photographs were taken in the hotel garden overlooking Dornoch Firth. Mr Gillespie, once the cost of Skibo Castle had been averted, had felt free to provide refreshments on a lavish scale. After a vinous lunch and some slightly incoherent speeches, the formal part of the event was over.

Grace had dressed for the ceremony in a knee-length dress of dusky cream silk, thus simultaneously and thriftily providing herself with a useful cocktail frock and sparing herself the difficulty of dancing in a long bridal gown. She had consented to carry at the ceremony a bouquet, which she had disposed of as soon as she decently could. Her one regret was that she had been pressed into wearing a matching hat with a small veil, which she could not imagine ever wearing again. That, too, she got rid of as soon as the formalities were over.

Mr Gillespie, combining extravagance with common sense, had reserved two reception rooms instead of the usual one. Those who wished to dance could do so in one room while in the other those preferring to chat could exchange news and gossip without having to shout. The groom, who was still walking with the aid of two sticks, was excused from dancing and so the bride, after submitting to her duty dances with the closer or more senior male guests, was free to kick off her uncomfortable shoes and rest her feet, settling at a corner table of the other room with May Largs. A waiter appeared out of nowhere and put down an opened bottle of Champagne.

May had graduated in horticulture and, after her marriage, had become a successful garden designer. During her years as a working gardener she had developed muscles which, now that she was specialising in design and leaving most of the physical labour to others, were in danger of turning to fat. She was engaged in a battle against this tendency by way of strict diets, exercises and compulsive labour in her own new garden. Her husband, a large man with no pretension to good looks, described her as 'pleasantly plump' and merely felt that he was getting more for his money. May's round face was innocent of makeup – her eyes were bright enough to need no embellishment – but her dark and usually rebellious curls seemed to have been given a severe talking-to.

Grace and Stuart were to settle in Stuart's house, almost directly across the Firth from the hotel. Because the house was already equipped with almost all that a newly wed couple could need and more than most could aspire to, wedding presents had posed a problem. The garden of Strathmore, however, ran to more than half an acre and had until recently been the province of Stuart's uncle, whose gardening talent had run more to patient cultivation than to imagination. Flowers and vegetables abounded but the formality of the layout, Grace said, reminded her of a suburban graveyard. An arrangement had been arrived at between May and Grace's parents. May would design and supervise a total overhaul ('Capability Brown rather than Inigo Jones,' she said) and the Gillespies would pay for the plants, materials and labour.

May's design was already finalised and the plants were on order, so that the time for serious discussion was past. Fuelled by Champagne and the occasion, they were laughing over suggestions involving garden gnomes, fountains, Astroturf and plastic daffodils when Jenny Welles, her duty done, joined them. Jenny was an attractive woman of vivid colouring, with black hair kept short – to keep it out of the camera's way, she always explained. She put an expensive-looking camera with its attendant flash carefully in the centre of the table and a glass of Champagne beside it. May and Jenny were friends, married to colleague policemen, and had arrived together from Beauly, near Inverness, by car. Her films, Jenny said, were already on the way to Inverness in the pocket of her motor-cycling cousin and should be printed and returned before the party broke up. If it ever broke up, she added, pouring wine.

'Steady on!' May said. 'You're driving.'

Jenny blinked at her. 'I thought you said that you were driving back.'

'I said that I wasn't.'

'But it's your turn. I drove to the Eden Court Theatre last week.'

'We weren't with you. We met you there.'

'It still counts.'

'Now, Children,' Grace said. 'No squabbles at my wedding. I don't see either of you driving all the way back or passing the breathalyser if you were stopped. I don't know what your respective husbands would say if you got yourselves fined and banned. And it's too far for a taxi. You can come home with Stuart and me, stay the night and one of us will run you back here in the morning. We have a taxi booked.'

'We could book into a hotel,' Jenny said half-heartedly.

'I doubt it. There's a golf tournament on as well as this shindig. We tried to get a last minute bed for one my uncles but everything was full. My mother's having to give him a shakedown.'

'In that case,' May said, 'we may as well enjoy the bubbly.' She topped up all three glasses. 'You're sure you don't mind us being with you on your bridal night.'

Grace looked at her with one eyebrow up – a habit that she had never been able to break. Although his injuries had formed only a minor impediment to the bridegroom's libido or ability, it seemed very unlikely that he would be capable of performing his conjugal duties after the drinks that, in true Highland tradition, were being forced on him. Surely her friends were not so naïve as to believe that tonight was to provide a first occasion?

'I thought you were supposed to be flying out to deepest Guatemala or somewhere tonight,' Jenny said.

'Aruba. And then a cruise ship. Yes, we were,' said Grace, 'but it's all gone haywire. You remember Stuart's uncle?'

'That awful old man? I'm sorry,' May said quickly. 'I shouldn't have said that.'

'Yes you should. You've described him to a nicety. I couldn't have put it better myself. Stuart remembers him as very affectionate and only a disciplinarian when it was called for. In fact, people keep telling me what a charmer he used to be, but nobody ever says what a charmer he is now. I never knew him until he'd turned into a grouchy old man, so I take any eulogies with a whole bucketful of salt.'

Jenny topped up all three glasses again. She was looking confused. 'I thought he was in hospital. Heart attack or something.'

'A stroke,' said Grace. 'A bad one. I didn't wish it on him, but it was a relief to think that he'd be off our hands at least until we came back. In fact, Stuart tried to do the gentlemanly thing and let me off my promise to marry him, just in case I found that I couldn't face up to the workload, but I told him that I was prepared to suffer the uncle for the nephew's sake and we had a highly emotional and very enjoyable scene over it. Anyway, they phoned from Raigmore earlier this week. They said that they needed every bed due to a superbug outbreak and that he was pining to go home. But I think that they were covering up. I think that the old – pardon my French – the old *bugger* saw his chance to muck us about. He's been on a good thing, living with Stuart, bossing him about and carrying on as if the house was his own. I wouldn't be surprised if he had a stroke on purpose so that Stuart and I couldn't boot him out.'

'You wouldn't really have done that, would you?' May asked.

'Probably not. Stuart certainly wouldn't. But his uncle hated the idea of Stuart marrying me and interfering with his little game so, out of spite, I think he made himself as objectionable to the nurses as only he can and now they can't wait to get rid of him. His speech is affected but he can get his message across when he wants to and he'd told them that I could postpone my *holiday*, would you believe? Not a word about my blessed honeymoon. They're booting him out, the day after tomorrow. Apparently there's an ambulance coming through to collect somebody who needs specialist care and he's coming with it. It's been hell on wheels rearranging everything.'

'I wouldn't have thought that it was possible,' May said.

'It wasn't, but I managed to change all the reservations around. We were supposed to have two weeks on Aruba and then a week's Caribbean cruise, but I managed to postpone the time in Aruba and bring the cruise forward by a week. So the islands we see won't be the ones we booked for, but I dare say they'll be just as much fun and with just the same sunshine. I couldn't get a short-term booking in a nursing home, so I phoned Mrs Gilchrist at the agency I used to work for and she's promised to send two nurses to live in until we come back.'

'Two?'

Grace looked up at the ceiling and made a face. 'I was lucky to get away with two. This isn't just home helping for some poor old body who can't get about as they used to. This is a cantankerous old bastard who's dumb and paralysed when he wants to be but manages to be a pain in the whatsit whenever he feels so inclined. And he's quite capable of choking or falling out of bed if he's left alone. Usually round-the-clock nursing takes three. But nurses don't expect to cook and clean for themselves. I've arranged for Hilda Munro, who lives almost next door, to look after them and sit in when needed. My mother's going to keep the puppy for us and she plans to call in from time to time and see that all's well.'

Jenny was pouring again. 'That's going to cost the earth.'

'It is,' Grace said. 'But you only get married once. Well, two or three times at the most. I'm hoping against hope that the order of business will be... nurses arrive, we leave, uncle comes home. But in the usual nature of things it will work out the other way around if it works out at all.'

'You still plan to be away for three weeks?' May asked. The music had started again but only reached them as a muffled beat.

'It's touch and go. The hotel wouldn't split a week but we could save a bit on the nurses if we came home early.'

'Work on your garden will have started before you come home. The nurses will love all the noise and disruption.'

'Tough!' said Grace. One of her cousins approached. She could not have refused his invitation to dance without starting a family feud, so she forced her feet into her shoes and rose reluctantly to her feet.

Chapter Two

Grace need not have worried. The two nurses arrived together in good time.

They were an ill-matched couple, yet they were friendly towards each other and usually nursed together, which did away with the ever-present danger of strife in that quarter. Janet Willoby was dark-haired and tall. She stood eye-to-eye with Grace, who was above average height. Janet carried herself well, an effect that was enhanced by a patrician nose usually held high. Alicia Kingsford, in contrast, was smaller and nicely rounded, with a snub nose and an eternally smiling face. She was also coloured, about the shade of café-au-lait, and her voice had the warm tone of the Caribbean. Neither looked more than thirty but Mrs Gilchrist had vouched for their skill and experience. They admired the house and, although Grace had warned them of the perils ahead, they pronounced themselves more than capable of coping with one recalcitrant stroke patient even while land-scaping work was carried out nearby.

Mr and Mrs Stuart Campbell flew out to enjoy their belated honeymoon with peaceful minds. Problems might await them on their return home, but for the moment they had only to take pleasure in each other and in their surroundings. The cruise ship was large enough to have all the amenities, small enough to be friendly. The cuisine was a danger to their waistlines. The ship wafted them in great comfort from one exotic harbour to another.

Laughter seemed to follow them. On their first night, 'Did you know,' Grace said, 'that you hum during sex?'

'Hum as in singing with the mouth closed? No, I didn't.'

'Well, you do. Just as we reach a climax, you hum the tune of "Here we go, here we go, here we go". And I'd rather that you didn't.'

'All right, I'll make a point of not.'

As they neared orgasm he was humming again. Grace recog-nised the tune of *The Campbells are coming*. She decided that she was marrying him for his sense of humour so she let it pass without comment; but the jiggle from her suppressed laughter added to their pleasure.

On the afterdeck of the cruise ship, by the pool, stood a statue of a young man, roughly life-size and the green colour of oxidised bronze. He stood on the tiptoes of one foot, his arms wide and his head back in an attitude of joyful abandon. He looked, Stuart said, as if he were trapped in an endless orgasm. Grace looked and it was true although the figure was seriously under-endowed in that respect. On the way to fetch drinks from the bar, to save Stuart managing with his sticks on the moving deck – and they were not, it may be said, the first drinks of the day – she paused by the statue. Temptation overcame her. On a mad and slightly fuddled impulse, she cupped her hands in line as though masturbating the green young man. As she looked, laughing, over her shoulder there came a ripple of laughter from other passengers. Stuart's camera was in his hands and there were other flashes blinking around the pool.

Grace, with all the dignity that she could still show, fetched the drinks and returned to Stuart. 'If you ever let anybody see that photograph,' she said, 'I'll put you back into the shape you were in when we first met.'

'Suppose I wait until I'm stronger than you are?'

Grace looked at him fondly. Although he seemed quite unaware of his looks, he was a very good-looking young man. He had perhaps looked slightly more swashbuckling when he still had the neat beard that suited him so well, but Grace had made severe comments about a beard smelling of nicotine. She had given him an ultimatum and he had sacrificed the beard rather than give up his very light smoking habit. He was well built and the symmetry of his body had been one of his first physical attractions for her; now she was working to return his musculature to the definition that had become blurred during his inactivity. 'Don't hold your breath,' she said. 'I work out. Do you want to arm-wrestle?'

Grace loved walking and her only regret was that Stuart was not yet fit enough to walk with her. But Aruba was hot and the scenery did not lend itself to walking. Swimming was the best possible exercise for Stuart's damaged joints, so he spent much of each day swimming gently in the shallows while Grace thrashed around in deeper water with much energy but at no great speed, each of them trying to work off the extra ounces deposited by the ship's cuisine. Then they covered each other with sunblock and watched the booby birds diving for sardines. Grace's dark blonde hair was turning golden under the sunshine.

In the evenings there was a cabaret and rum-based cocktails. Morning and night, Grace worked to complete the repairs to Stuart's injuries. By early in the second week, he could walk without his sticks although he felt safer with at least one in his hand. He was demonstrating his prowess across the bedroom floor when the bedside telephone rang. Grace rolled over and picked it up. Even when she heard her mother's voice on the line, she felt no qualms. Mrs Gillespie had phoned several times to check on their safe arrival, Stuart's progress and Grace's satisfaction with the married state, each of which had been satisfactory.

This time, however, Mrs Gillespie forewent the inquisition. Unusually for her, she came straight to the point. 'I hate to spoil your honeymoon, Grace, but you'll have to come back.'

Grace had just awoken from the deep sleep of the much loved and she was in no mood for sudden drama. 'I am going to come back, Mother. At the end of next week.'

'No, dear. I mean now. Right away. Those nurses are threatening to walk out.'

Grace woke up very quickly with a sudden fluttering in her abdomen. Back in Scotland, life was still real and earnest. 'They'll get their licenses withdrawn if they leave a patient in the lurch.'

'I told them that. They seem to feel that that would be the lesser evil.'

Well, that was one way of looking at it, but not one that Grace was prepared to admit. 'Phone Mrs Gilchrist. I left her number with you. Get two more.'

'I tried. She says it could take a week or two and I don't think we've got that long.'

'Any particular reason for the walkout?'

'Several. The most pressing seems to be that he's been making passes at them. They say that they daren't come within reach of his good hand any more. They have to do everything from his bad side.'

Grace was well aware that when a patient loses ability for most of his or her enthusiasms, these may find surprising outlets in other areas. All the same... 'Mother, that doesn't sound like Stuart's uncle at all. He's an obsessive puritan. Are you sure that they delivered the right Mr Cameron?'

'They must have, dear. He's been visited by members of his club. They'd surely have said.'

Grace was still too languorous to make sudden decisions. 'Practised nurses should be able to cope with that sort of thing. I'll talk it over with Stuart and call you back.'

Grace talked it over with Stuart. He kissed the tip of her nose and said, 'We could call their bluff and stick to the programme. They wouldn't really walk out.'

'They might. I probably would, if I didn't have the incentive of a loving husband.'

'Do whatever you think is best. I'll be sorry to leave here early, but we've had a great time and I feel ready to face the rigors of home whenever you are.'

She phoned Mrs Gilchrist, but the availability of nurses was much as Grace's mother had stated. She phoned Strathmore, Stuart's house (she did not yet think of it as "home"). Janet Willoby answered.

'What's this I hear about two of you not being to cope with one old man?' Grace demanded.

Janet had seemed imperturbable but she was undoubtedly perturbed now. Her voice, usually calm with a smooth Oxbridge accent, was shaking. 'Oh, Miss Gillespie, I should say Mrs Campbell, we hate to let down a client and especially a colleague, and on your honeymoon too, but put up with this sort of behaviour we can not and will not do any longer. I mean, we've nursed psychopaths and deviants and I even had a patient once who thought he could pee over the moon, but how anyone whose speech is as badly affected as your uncle's —'

'My husband's uncle,' Grace corrected. She had no intention of leaving room for misapprehensions on that score.

'Sorry. But how anyone whose speech is so badly affected can be so rude and make such suggestions I don't know. And, not to put too fine a point on it, the groping...'

Grace sighed and uttered words that were to haunt her. 'I swear I'll kill the old bastard. Put some bromide in his tea.'

'We tried that. It seems to make him worse. You see, it isn't physical, it's emotional.'

Grace sighed again, more deeply. Stuart's uncle had never married and it seemed that the frustrated urges of a lifetime spent partly at sea and partly living with and setting an example to his nephew were now freed from the control of his damaged brain. 'You do realise,' she said, 'that the old devil hated the idea of Stuart and me marrying? He's probably just playing you up out of spite. Do you want him to win?'

'Honestly,' Janet said, 'I think he's already won, whether he knows it or not. I don't think he's as rational as you suggest, or only sometimes. It comes and goes.'

'Raigmore had no business discharging him in that condition,' Grace said hotly.

'No. But the alternative would probably have been to have him sectioned. And I'll tell you something else. That doctor's a bum-pincher.'

'Is he really? He's never laid a finger on me.'

'He wouldn't. Not if you're his patient.'

Grace recalled that she had obtained a prescription for bendrofluazide from the doctor. She thought furiously. One of her favourite comedians made frequent reference to a Maximum Security Twilight Home, but she knew of no such convenient repository, failing which... 'All right,' she said, 'we'll come home as quickly as we possibly can. Hang on until then.'

'Well, we'll try,' Janet said. 'But we may have to call on a squad of strong, male neighbours whenever he needs a bath.'

'Do that. Pay them if you have to,' Grace said. 'We'll refund you.'

Grace and Stuart had reached the Caribbean in two flights and in a single day, although the day had been stretched by the time-change. It took them four days and five flights to return home, and much extra expenditure. Seats were not always available on the most suitable flights, especially in Tourist class. To add to their difficulties, their honeymoon had been timed to suit Stuart's determination to be back in harness before the start of the new school year, which meant that the hurricane season was at its height. Hurricane Geoffrey was swerving around the Caribbean and threatening parts of the Eastern Seaboard of the USA. Planes were diverted or never took off. Frustration reigned supreme.

They had elected to start their journeying from Glasgow, where Stuart's estate car could be left in secure storage. They finally made it back to Glasgow, scruffy and exhausted, early on the Monday morning, almost exactly when they had been scheduled to return anyway. For most of the journey, they had been afraid to move to a hotel in case a delayed flight might be suddenly called or seats become available; and they had slept on planes or in a variety of airport lounges. They had become separated from their main luggage.

There was no sign of their luggage at Glasgow. Not aware that it had managed to reach Glasgow more than a day ahead of them, they wasted time leaving messages and instructions against its eventual arrival. They collected the car. During their absence the weather had broken. The A9 was crowded and heavy vehicles were throwing up bow-waves of spray. Stuart was still not yet supple enough to take over the driving. Grace suggested pulling off for a meal at North Kessock, but they decided that hot baths and sleep had a higher priority.

As they crossed the Cromarty Firth, the rain stopped. They took the short cut over the hills from Alness. The familiar hills began to soothe away their troubles. They were almost within sight of Dornoch Firth when they came on forestry works. For half an hour, they waited while vehicles and machinery wove incomprehensible patterns in front of them.

The car was stuffy. Stuart wound down a window but he soon wound it up again. 'It's cold,' he said.

Grace looked at the dashboard thermometer. 'An ordinary,

cool summer's day here. We're too used to a warmer clime.'

'Well, it seems cold to me. Fit to freeze the balls off a brass monkey.'

Grace was developing a headache and it was making her irritable. 'I've never understood that expression. Why balls? Why monkey? And why use rude expressions when technically, I suppose, we're still on our honeymoon?'

As home came closer, Stuart was relaxing more. 'It isn't rude. I'll explain. In the days of cannon and sailing ships, it was normal to keep a stack of thirty cannonballs beside each gun; but if the bottom layer could roll they'd all roll. So the bottom square, four each way, was fitted into a metal plate with sixteen hollows to keep the bottom layer of balls in place. To prevent them rusting into place the plate, which was known as a "monkey", was made of brass. But brass has a higher coefficient of thermal expansion and contraction than iron, so that in very cold weather the brass monkey would contract to the point at which the cannonballs began to roll off. There now. I bet you didn't know that.'

But Grace was asleep.

At last, a man with a flag waved them through. Stuart nudged Grace awake and they came down to the road along the south side of Dornoch Firth. Ten minutes later, they reached home at Strathmore, one of a row of three small houses in otherwise unbroken countryside. The driveway was obstructed by two cars, some materials for the remodelling of the garden and a skip containing the superseded and uprooted plants and shrubs, but the pair were ravenous and demoralised and Grace had a pounding headache, so she crammed the car in any old how.

Their luggage had been delivered and was stacked in the hall and it seemed at first that the worst might be over. There was, however, a babble of raised voices coming from Duncan Cameron's room.

'Leave this to me,' Grace said grimly.

'He's my uncle. Perhaps I should…'

'You're too used to knuckling down to him,' Grace said. 'You wouldn't have the heart to tell him where he gets off. Put the kettle on and a pan for poached eggs or something and I'll give you an expurgated version later.'

Stuart hesitated and then nodded sadly. 'There's something in what you say. He was father and mother to me for years.' He went into the kitchen.

Grace squared her shoulders and walked into the old man's room. The scene that awaited her would have been suited to a Hogarth etching. A throng of ladies, which she later identified as comprising the two nurses, her own mother and Hilda Munro from next door but one, was registering, in their various manners, shock and horror. Duncan Cameron, twisted by his stroke but still unmistakably venomous, was in bed but struggling against many restraining hands to rise. His old fashioned nightshirt was up and his withered genitalia were exposed. Janet Willoby had been right – his excitement was only in his mind.

Grace had had enough and more than enough. She stepped forward. The old man's eyes lit on her and she thought that she could detect a momentary gleam of triumph, immediately fading. She stooped until she was nose to nose with him and glared.

Stuart did not hear what she said. Grace could never remember her own words and the ladies who had been in the room refused to repeat any of them, but what she said cut through the fog clouding the old man's mind. Pouting like a smacked child, Stuart's uncle settled back on the pillows and was immediately made decent and tucked in with a firmness that must surely, Grace thought, have inhibited his breathing.

Grace was tempted to enquire whether she had had to come all the way back from Aruba just for that. But she decided in time that to capitalise on her triumph might rebound, once the shock effect had worn off. That question, moreover, was already hanging unvoiced in the air of the room and to ask it at all would have lessened its impact.

Chapter Three

To the great relief of the ladies, Duncan Cameron soon succumbed to his medication and fell asleep. The time was more than ripe for some discussion of future arrangements. Mrs Gillespie and Miss Munro agreed to watch over the patient while the two nurses accompanied Grace to the kitchen.

Grace had been looking forward to getting the kitchen, which had been Duncan Cameron's province, to herself. It was of a generous size, very well equipped and, for all his faults, the old man had always kept it spotless. The ladies who had had charge of it during Grace's absence on honeymoon did not seem to have let the standard slip. The picture window over the sink and worktop looked over the spreading back garden, where the neatly regimented beds had been torn apart and were being replaced by May's informal design. Five or six men were hard at work. Several gardening machines were standing by but Grace was pleased to note that the half-dozen men were at work with spades in comparative quiet. The rain had not reached so far north and the sky was clearing. The view extended across Dornoch Firth to where the shadows of the breaking clouds wandered across the hills beyond. Grace could almost make out the house, two miles away, where she had been born and had lived for her first five years. It was no more than a roof peeping above the trees but soon, when the leaves fell, she would be able on a clear day to see what had once been her nursery window.

Stuart, well versed in the ways of womenfolk, had brewed tea in his largest teapot and Alicia carried two cups through to the patient's room. The nurses had eaten but were agreeable to drinking tea and nibbling fancy biscuits while Stuart and Grace tackled large mixed grills of eggs, bacon, venison sausages, tomatoes and what Grace judged to be the finest bread ever fried. 'Heart Attack Heaven,' Stuart called it, but the two, who had subsisted almost entirely on airline and airport food for several days, were past caring. Good tea, properly made with the water freshly boiling, was a bonus.

Discussion began only when Grace and Stuart's tans had been

properly admired and even then it was punctuated by long gaps for chewing and swallowing, allowing Grace time for thought. Their courtship had been reaching its culmination when Stuart's uncle suffered his stroke. Grace had originally come to Strathmore as Stuart's physiotherapist but she had ample nursing experience. As she had told her friends at the wedding reception, she had dismissed Stuart's reservations, insisting that she would be well able to tend a patient and keep house. But now, she was beginning to wonder. A passive patient would have been manageable but a venomous and recalcitrant one was going to pose a problem that would only be chased away by throwing money at it – and money might soon be in short supply.

She emptied her mouth and, while she spoke, she used the interval to add mustard to a slice of sausage. 'So you want to chicken out and leave me to struggle on alone?' she asked.

The two nurses were defensive. Alicia spoke first. Her warm, Jamaican tones reminded Grace of voices heard during her enforced halts in the Caribbean. Her brown eyes were earnest. 'We tried giving him a good talking to,' she said. 'It didn't work for us.'

'Probably not,' said Grace. 'You have to be genuinely angry. Like being fetched back from your honeymoon.'

Both nurses flinched. 'Be fair to us,' Janet pleaded. 'Imagine the worst patient in the world and then think of somebody much, much worse, and that's him. I'm sorry,' she added to Stuart.

'Don't apologise,' Stuart said. 'I wouldn't have expected anything different. Honest to God, I can only ask you to believe that he's changed. He used to be the kindliest old chap you could meet, a favourite uncle to every child and courtly to the ladies without ever stepping over the line. As he got older he turned into a thrawn old devil and this stroke seems to have removed all his inhibitions. All the wickedness that he was suppressing for years is pouring out.'

'So at least we're agreed about that,' Grace said. 'What else can we agree?'

The two nurses exchanged a glance. 'We're due to be paid up to the end of the week,' said Janet. 'Now that you're here to help control him, we don't mind staying on that long, but we draw the line at bedbaths and most definitely at suppositories.' She glanced at Alicia, who nodded assent.

Grace was on the point of arguing that if they abandoned their posts because they were unable to cope with one elderly gentleman, they could abandon the remuneration as well. But she was distracted. 'Suppositories?'

'His bowel movements are affected,' Alicia explained. 'His doctor arranged for some suppositories and the commode.'

'He could be faking it,' said Janet austerely. 'He seems treat it as a rather erotic game. It's a game that we definitely do not enjoy playing but that only seems to add to his enjoyment. We give him one after his breakfast every morning and then help him onto the commode. He seems to prefer that to a bedpan.'

Grace told herself firmly that the Victorian attitude had been mistaken. What gave somebody pleasure was not necessarily sinful. But she found the argument, when applied to suppositories, unconvincing and repellent. 'I'll take over the suppositories and help with the bedbaths,' she said bravely, 'if you'll see out the week. By then I'll hope to have developed a routine, come to an arrangement with the district nurse and spoken to the NHS about some home help.'

'Failing which,' Stuart said, 'Raigmore can have him back, whether they want him or not. He's my uncle and I owe him a lot, but I'm not having my wife run ragged.'

Grace's headache was abating under the benign influence of food, tea and no longer being in motion. She was more ready to compromise. 'Thank you for that, my dear, but I'll be the judge of what I can manage. I don't usually gave a damn what people say about me, but I'll not have them saying that you got rid of your uncle as soon as you had a wife to look after you.'

'Which is all very well,' said Janet, 'but do you really have room for everybody?'

She had a point. Duncan Cameron was occupying the largest of the bedrooms. Stuart and Grace had planned to settle in Stuart's old room. The spare room was smaller and had only a three-quarter sized bed.

'You see,' Alicia said, 'we never share a room. We don't mind working together. We make a good team. But not sharing a room is the one thing that we never compromise on. It's because each of us thinks that the other snores. We may even both be right.' Her smile flashed white in her dark face.

'And my uncle doesn't need a night-nurse?' Stuart asked.

'No.' Janet shook her head. 'The doctor gave us some pills for him. He sleeps through. And we have a baby-alarm.'

'Would you hear him, if his speech is affected?'

'It's affected, not silenced,' Janet said grimly. 'We'd hear him all right.'

'Hang on a minute.' Grace got up. She crossed the hall to Duncan Cameron's room and looked in.

Mrs Gillespie was alone. Grace's eye was caught by a photograph in a leather frame. It showed an attractive young woman in a good but dated dress. 'That's new,' she said. 'Who is it?

'I never saw her in my life. We found it in a drawer and thought that it might cheer him up.' They moved out into the hall. 'Hilda Munro went home to see to her brother's dinner,' Mrs Gillespie said. 'I'm holding the fort. But don't be too long. Your father will be coming in-by to collect me, any minute.' She gave a little shiver. 'I'll be glad to get out of here. It hurts to see Mr Cameron sunk to this. He used to be such a sweet man. One used to meet him around when he was ashore and in some quite good houses. He had beautiful manners. I don't know where he picked them up.'

'Stuart told me that his uncle did some of his naval service on the royal yacht.' Grace looked at her watch. 'He'd have to start with good manners to be chosen for that service and it would go on from there. I'll make it quick, then. I've persuaded the nurses to stay on for the week. Can Stuart and I come to stay with you again for that long? There just isn't the room here. We'd be out all day, not under your feet.'

Mrs Gillespie beamed. 'Yes, of course. We'll love having you both again.' There was the sound of an expensive car horn from the road. 'There's your father now.' She touched her head. 'I've left my hat in there. When can we expect you?'

'As soon as we've sorted things out here.'

'You'll be needing an evening meal then?'

Grace thought quickly. Happy as she was to be home – and at last she was thinking of Strathmore as home – the house was crowded and the peace disturbed. Her hunger was temporarily assuaged but Stuart would certainly be ravenous again in an hour or so. The idea of escaping to a tranquil house and a good meal cooked by somebody else held immense appeal. 'We'd love it. Say hello to Dad for me and we'll see him later.'

'Yes, of course.' Mrs Gillespie looked at her daughter anxiously. 'I didn't like to ask you on the phone, but was everything all right? You know? *That* way.'

Grace looked round to be sure that the kitchen door was closed. 'Mother, everything was marvellous, *that* way.'

'Even with Stuart's injuries?'

'Yes, even with his injuries.'

'I thought, perhaps, with the damage to his elbows...'

Grace tried not to giggle. She was tempted to say that not every gentleman takes his weight on his elbows. 'Mother, that didn't bother us the least little bit.'

'That's all right then. I'd better get to the shops. It'll have to be something that doesn't take too long.' The horn sounded again. 'I must go.' She turned to the front door.

'Mother. Your hat.'

'Yes, of course.'

They entered the sickroom together.

Duncan Cameron had managed somehow to get from between the sheets and to balance on his better leg. With an air of grim triumph, he was urinating into Mrs Gillespie's hat.

'I never liked that hat much anyway,' Mrs Gillespie said faintly.

Chapter Four

Before Grace reached her teens, her parents had moved to a roomy house in Dornoch looking over the golf course and towards the sea. Except that she now shared her bedroom with a husband, it was as though she had never been away. Grace's mother was happy to look after them as she felt a mother should. Grace, who had managed for herself for years or endured other peoples' houses, enjoyed the cosseting. Instead of coming down to earth after his honeymoon, Stuart, who was becoming immersed in preparations to resume his teaching career, was vaguely aware that he was eating better than he ever had when his uncle had charge of the catering and that his nights were no longer lonely or disturbed by erotic dreams.

One of their wedding presents formed a welcome intrusion into their new lives. Grace's brother, now living in Inverness, had, after consultation, given her a highly pedigreed golden retriever bitch puppy. Her lengthy kennel-name, in Gaelic, had been abandoned for home use in favour of Bonzo, which sounded slightly similar to the first two syllables in the Gaelic name. At ten weeks, Bonzo was a charming and entertaining bundle of fur, obviously hugely intelligent (at least in the eyes of her new owners) and eager to please. Grace had great fun getting to know her new friend and beginning the first stages of elementary training with the aid of several textbooks and a whole range of training equipment.

During the day, Bonzo had to remain in the care of Mrs Gillespie. Strathmore was too busy and too close to the road for a puppy to run loose while doors and gates stood open and nobody had time to keep watch. Grace and Stuart found their time full. Grace's car had been written off after a smash and the insurance money had disappeared along with most of her savings. Her parents had spent enough on her wedding without being asked to help out with her trousseau, and Grace had born her share of the cost of flying home ahead of tickets that had been prepaid. Stuart had protested that these costs were his responsibility because it was his uncle who was the cause of the extra costs, but Grace, though uncomfortably aware that she was unlikely to contribute much to the joint exchequer, was determined to pull as much of her weight as she could for as long as possible. Later, when she had to look after Stuart's uncle single-handed, a car of her own would become essential; but for the moment Stuart could drop her at Strathmore in the morning and collect her later in the day by an acceptable deviation from his way home from the school. Duncan Cameron's car was lying idle in the garage, but Grace had no way of obtaining the owner's permission to drive it and was fairly sure that such permission would be refused even if she managed to communicate with him. Anyway the car was old and disreputable. Grace was not proud, but there were limits.

To what extent the old man was "swinging the lead", Grace could not decide. He could overcome his paralysis to a remarkable degree when he really wanted to, such as when putting his cold and bony hand where it would not be welcomed; but when asked to assist in any activity that he disliked, he became limp and comatose. Similarly, he might often be lost for words in normal communication but usually, after some delay and obvious mental effort, he could summon up an approximation to words of complaint or abuse in terms which would never have passed his lips during his days as an ardent churchgoer. His language and sentiments might be stumbling but they were not moderated even when members of his kirk visited him. The minister in particular had made a rapid escape, very pink about the ears. When Mr Cameron called Alicia a nigger to her face, the departure of both nurses was only averted by Grace's quick pretence that he had been asking for a *bigger* something-or-other. The explanation had been accepted, if not wholly believed.

The old man seemed to be in some awe of Grace. After the death of Stuart's parents, his uncle had been his guardian and mentor. While Duncan Cameron's naval service lasted, he had been a longed-for father figure, returning regularly with gifts and treats. After his retirement, he could almost be said to have devoted his life to his nephew's wellbeing. The habits of both deference and gratitude died hard and Stuart could not bring himself to speak sharply to him even when the old man was being his most outrageous. Grace, however, had arrived in Stuart's house as Stuart's nurse and physiotherapist and she had not been prepared to stand any nonsense.

A *modus vivendi* was quickly re-established at Strathmore. The nurses continued to look after the patient provided only that Grace was present as a restraining influence during such activities as ablutions, evacuation or the insertion of the daily suppository. The arrangement provided a satisfactory compromise. The patient was sufficiently in awe of Grace that she could minister to him while wearing a skirt without fear of a cold and wandering hand up it, whereas the nurses came on duty in trousers.

This regime allowed Grace some time to get the house into order and to pursue arrangements for managing when the nurses made their departure. In this respect the NHS was for once helpful and it began to look as though some degree of home help might be available. Grace did some sums, based on the hope that she might be able to take on some private physiotherapy patients. She began to watch the advertisements, looking for a dealer who was offering interest-free car credit.

By the Wednesday after their return, the nurses were nearing the end of their engagement. By then, Grace could envisage life in a busy but comfortable routine, with Stuart's uncle stable and more or less under control, the work of looking after him being shared with Grace by visiting helpers provided or at least sub-sidised by the NHS.

That morning, the doctor called. Dr Sullivan was a small and tubby man but he had kept most of his silver hair. He was begin-ning to run down his share of the workload in the practice in preparation for an early retirement, which he intended to take while he could still enjoy his golf, fishing, curling and other unspecified pastimes. He still attended to a number of favoured or longstanding patients. It seemed that he was taking into his retirement an element of youthful vigour. Grace had known him when he was Stuart's doctor after the fall. Like Duncan Cameron in earlier days, he had a charming manner to women. Grace's mother had warned her to be wary of the doctor or else to become his patient. The doctor, she whispered, was said to have affairs with unattached ladies away from his practice. He also had a tendency to be over familiar with his women patients but there had never been any suggestion that he stepped over the bounds of professional propriety. As a doctor he was considered more than merely capable.

Duncan Cameron had been particularly agitated that morning but the doctor's visit had a tranquillising effect. Stuart's uncle seemed to remember him and calmed down while the doctor tapped and prodded, shone a torch into his eyes, sounded his chest and listened to his heart and lungs. Then Grace and Janet took the doctor into the sitting room. The patient had been given his suppository and Alicia was watching over him. She would call for help at the first sign of activity, but with the patient's functions affected by stubbornness and paralysis, this could often take a surprisingly long time. The mutter of machinery filtered in from the garden. As hostess, Grace fetched coffee.

'I gather that I've come at a bad time,' the doctor said, stirring thoughtfully.

'Or a good one,' Grace said, 'depending on which way you look at it. He may need to be sedated. Today, for the first time, they're using machinery in the garden and it seemed to dawn on him, also for the first time, that changes were being made without his agreement.' She made a face. 'If he'd been physically capable of hitting the ceiling, he'd have hit it.'

'We've been trying to calm him down,' Janet said. 'It only seems to make him worse. It's not easy to make out what he's trying to say, but he got his message across. He's not a happy bunny.'

'His room's at the front of the house,' Grace explained, 'the same as this one, so even when we sat him up he never saw the garden except for the little bit this side, which isn't being touched. But my parents gave us a makeover of the main garden for a wedding present and May Largs did the design.'

'I've seen some of her work,' said the doctor. 'She's good. But I thought the house and garden belonged to your husband.'

'They do,' Grace said. 'But try saying that to his uncle. The old man's been looking after the garden for years and years and he's put a lot of work into it. Flowers everywhere and a few vegetables – and never a weed to be seen, to do him justice. But it was all in squares with edgings and neat paths and no attention given to height or to harmonious colours. If you looked into any one of the beds it pleased the eye, but looked at overall it was like a rather gaudy tartan – the Hunting McGinsberg, perhaps – and just about as natural. And the only place to sit out was at the gable of the house, where you only get the sun in the middle of the day. May's giving us a bit of a terrace, a wandering sort of lawn and some easily kept beds with trees and shrubs against the boundaries.

'Everyone mucked in and tried to set it up so that most of the work would be done while we were away on our honeymoon. We didn't expect Raigmore to get fed up and kick him out. We've tried to kid him that we only have some gardeners in to prepare the beds for next year because he isn't fit to do the work, but he isn't buying it. He's fizzing.'

'Dear oh dear!' said the doctor. 'I'd better have another look at him.'

'Perhaps you'd better wait,' Janet said. 'He's had his suppository. After that's worked, he's usually tired and more manageable.'

Doctor Sullivan nodded and settled back into his chair. 'I still think it would have been better to send him to the Newcraigs Psychiatric Hospital in Inverness. There's no stigma attached to such places any more.'

'The suggestion still has its attractions,' Grace said unhappily, 'but, looking at it from the patient's viewpoint, it would be cruel. His mind isn't all there, but he'd understand that his life here was over. It would break his miserable old heart. We'll save that for a desperate last…'

She was interrupted by a call for help from Alicia. Grace led the way into the patient's room. Alicia was stooped over the bed, attempting resuscitation by heart massage. She stood back to let the doctor work. 'He seemed to be overtaken by a sudden fit,' Alicia said. She sounded tearful. 'I was out of the room for a few minutes, just to go to the toilet. When I came back, something was wrong. He gasped several times and then he just stopped breathing. I did what I could.'

'I'm sure you did,' Grace said. This was not the first time that she had been at the death of a patient, but the old man's relationship to Stuart gave the prospect of death a poignancy.

'Can I help?' she asked the doctor. A horrid smell was permeating the room and she was sure that there was nothing she could possibly do.

The doctor straightened up and folded his stethoscope. He touched a clouding eye and then closed both eyelids. 'No heartbeat,' he said. 'No breathing. No reaction whatever to external stimuli. He's gone. Another stroke, surely. Perhaps it's just as well. Stroke patients can make remarkable recoveries, but in his case the damage was much too severe. He would never have walked again or spoken clearly. Perhaps it's kinder this way. A peaceful death is often easier than lingering on. If he'd been a favourite dog, we'd have had no hesitation in putting him to sleep when it first happened but people are forbidden that final privilege. If I said that in public I'd be ostracised, but in medical company it can be said aloud.' He smiled sadly and patted Grace's shoulder. 'I'll make out a death certificate. You can collect it from my office. Contact me again if I can help in any other way.'

'Thank you.' Grace saw him to the door. 'You did all that was possible,' she said. 'I'll come over in a day or two for the certificate.'

The doctor looked up at the sun, which was struggling through a thin layer of cloud. 'I always feel so guilty, somehow,' he said. He eased himself into his car and backed carefully out into the road.

The two nurses were already engaged in cleaning up the body as a final service to their patient. Grace was free to phone Stuart at the school and tell him that his uncle had passed away. Stuart took the news quietly and there was a short silence on the line. 'That's it, then,' he said at last.

'I'm afraid so. Don't be too sad.'

'I'm not,' Stuart said after a few seconds of thought. He

sounded slightly surprised. 'It surely can't have been a pleasurable existence, paralysed like that. It's better this way.'

'The doctor said something very similar.'

'He was right. And it does relieve me of the worry of wondering how you'll cope. I'll come home.'

'You needn't,' Grace told him. 'The house is full of nurses tidying up. There's nothing you could do except mope and get in the way. At the school, you're doing something useful as depute head, getting ready for next term, and it'll keep your mind occupied. Just tell me which undertaker you want to use and I'll phone them for you.'

When she put the phone down, although she could hear the two nurses giving the patient their final attention, the house seemed very quiet. It was as though it knew that somebody who had once been happy in it had gone at last. She tried to be sad but sadness wouldn't come. It seemed appropriate somehow to go out to the skip and salvage the last of the flowers. When the vases were filled with a motley collection of colours, she settled down at the phone and began the long processes that follow a death in the family.

Chapter Five

Most of us subconsciously reject the idea of our own mortality. Thus the average death leaves behind a mountain of odds and ends – all those things laid aside in case they might prove useful next week and then forgotten. All of these have to be sifted through. There may be clues to forgotten investments or to wishes not embodied in any will. While Stuart began to sort his uncle's property into bags for the rubbish, boxes for the worthwhile and a folder to be delivered to the manager of an Inverness building society who was named as his uncle's executor, Grace borrowed her husband's car and drove to the surgery.

In a sparsely populated area the villages tend to be small. There was no single village large enough to support a modern practice. Dr Sullivan had solved the problem by settling in a small village central to other villages and to a rural catchment area. He had built a smart new surgery close to the bus stop where his more elderly patients could easily reach him. High window sills allowed privacy during examinations; the doctor and his partners had protested vigorously and successfully when the use of double-decker buses had been proposed. The low structure of brick and tile had been objected to by many of the locals on the ground that the materials were not native to the area but Grace, who had learned to appreciate a variety of architecture, recognised the bricks as being facing bricks of high quality. The building had by its nature to differ in scale, shape and style from its neighbours, from which it was separated by margins of grass and shrubs, and Grace liked it – a view which was gradually gaining general acceptance.

Grace had intended to say a few words of thanks to the doctor for his attendance and help and perhaps to ask what he had meant when he had mentioned feeling guilty. If the words had signified that he always felt guilty when he failed to keep a patient alive indefinitely, perhaps the doctor was himself in need of reassurance. But there had been an accident on one of the farms, the farmer getting his hand trapped in the mechanism of a tractor, and the doctor had been called out, so the question remained unasked. Grace was left to suppose that to lose a patient must always, to a doctor, seem like failure.

The death certificate had been left with the practice receptionist. Miss Dawburn was a retired nurse; indeed, Grace recalled that when she had been a pupil at Dornoch Academy Miss Dawburn had been the school nurse. She was now definitely on the verge of her use-by date, but although her figure had thickened she had not let it go. Her dress was carefully chosen but would have better suited a woman fifteen years younger. Her hair, fluffy enough to disguise any tendency to thinness, was still fair although Grace suspected that the natural colour had faded. All in all, Miss Dawburn managed to present to the first glance a picture of a woman not yet beyond the age for dalliance. And the best of luck to her, Grace thought in the patronising way of the safely wed. Why should the young have a monopoly of romance? Their elders, being unlikely to add to the world's already excessive population, had the greater right.

Retaining only the aspirin, Grace had collected Duncan Cameron's medications into a small cardboard box and brought them to the surgery for disposal. Miss Dawburn pushed them to a corner of her desk. The death certificate was in front of her, but instead of handing it over she gave Grace a chair and a cup of tea and settled down for a cosy chat. 'Very sad, Mr Cameron's death,' she said.

Grace was uncertain how to reply. Duncan Cameron's death might have seemed sad to himself, although even that was open to doubt. To Stuart it probably marked the close of an era that was already ending. To everyone who had had dealings with him in recent years it had come as a blessed relief. She hunted for an answer and found one that was suitably noncommittal. 'It was inevitable,' she said.

'Of course, of course.' Miss Dawburn seemed well satisfied with the comment. She got up to direct a young mother with attached infant to a seat in the waiting room. She put a tick against an appointment and sat down again. 'But I'm sure that Doctor Sullivan did everything possible. Such a pity! Such a charming man!'

'The doctor? Or my uncle by marriage?'

Miss Dawburn showed confusion. 'Why, both of them,' she said. 'The doctor is always charming. But I meant Mr Cameron.'

Although she had heard it rather often, Grace was hard put to it to recognise this as a description of the late Mr Cameron as she had known him. 'When did you last see him?' she asked.

Miss Dawburn thought about that. 'It must be years,' she said. 'Not since the doctor sent him for an operation on —' she lowered her voice – 'his prostate. He was very hale. He hardly ever seemed to need the doctor up until his stroke. He was always the gentleman, very neatly dressed, and when he spoke to a lady she knew that he wasn't thinking of someone else, she was sort of special to him. Doctor Sullivan is just the same. That was what I meant by charm.' She stopped, flustered.

If Miss Dawburn was remembering Duncan Cameron during his earlier, gentler days, Grace was glad. It was proper that somebody beside his nephew should remember him kindly. She recalled that Miss Dawburn had always been the first to detect charm and romantic possibilities in any unmarried male. The arrival of the practise nurse, who came to get the key of the drug cupboard from Miss Dawburn's keeping, saved Grace from having to reply directly. 'Perhaps that's what we all mean by charm,' she said. 'It's all been very upsetting.'

'I'm sure. And is there any other news?'

Grace was puzzled. Surely the other couldn't be enquiring as to whether she was already pregnant. 'None at all,' she said firmly.

'When somebody dies, there are always consequences. Things that affect other people, I mean. I suppose your husband comes into his uncle's house now?'

This was so far out of line that Grace was almost tempted into downright rudeness. But she might well need medical favours in the future, or to have her name suggested to possible clients seeking physiotherapy. 'The house has always belonged to Stuart,' she said firmly. 'Could I have the death certificate, please. The undertaker's waiting for it.'

The doctor's receptionist was not going to be put off. 'Has the will been read?'

Grace kept her temper. 'The will was in a sealed envelope. The name of the executor was on the envelope so we delivered it to him. He'll be wanting a copy of the death certificate, if you'll just let me have it. That's all I know.' Grace decided that Miss Dawburn had earned a dig in return. 'Why? Were you expecting a legacy?' The receptionist tried to look coy. 'Was there something special between you?'

Miss Dawburn looked scandalised and yet, in a perverse way, pleased. 'Certainly not! How could you suggest such a thing? Mr Cameron was old enough to be my father.'

Grace considered striking the final blow by looking doubtful as to the veracity of that last statement but decided to be merciful. Miss Dawburn would be well aware of the difference in ages between herself and Stuart's uncle. She gathered up the death certificate while the other was distracted and made her escape.

The funeral was held on the following Monday. In addition to her often voiced reservations about organised religion, Grace objected strongly to the process of burial, deeming it to be a waste of precious land, productive of morbid landscapes, unhygienic and in a way disrespectful in leaving the abandoned human shell to rot. She also felt that the regular visits, necessary if the plot were not to fall into disgraceful ruin, were an imposition on the living, who would probably remember the deceased with greater affection if not obliged to carry out that depressing duty. Mr Cameron's desire to be buried near his late sister at a small country church near Tain, the area of his birth, had been well known and Grace was torn. Attending the funeral was against her principles. On the other hand, she had no desire to appear disrespectful, especially to any of her new in-laws.

Duncan Cameron had not remained popular with his relatives. Stuart and his uncle had not belonged to a prolific family and, of those relatives still living, most were too distant to attend and had sent flowers and apologies. In contrast, however, there was a full attendance from his various clubs, from the congregation of his church and of past colleagues. The small church was part-way to seeming crowded.

The nurses, Alicia and Janet, were there to pay their respects. They were not contracted to start another assignment for some time and they had taken a liking to the area. They had no permanent homes of their own and lived much the same peripatetic life as Grace had once lived. Grace and Stuart wanted to move back into Strathmore. The nurses' first enquiries for suitable bed-and-breakfast accommodation had been dealt with quickly. Janet was granted extended use of the Campbells' spare room. Until the late Mr Cameron's room was cleared and available for guests, Alicia was to stay with Hilda Munro and her brother, almost next door. Hilda arrived at the church with her brother George. They were usually dependent on George's motorbike and sidecar, but this was not felt to be a respectful way to arrive at a funeral so they had begged a lift with Alicia. Miss Dawburn arrived with the doctor.

The usual funeral tones of black and dark grey were relieved by splashes of bright colour. In the Highlands, the kilt is considered suitably respectful garb for a burying. Many of the faces were half familiar to Grace, shadows from her youth, but seeing them out of context and in unfamiliar clothes she could not put names to half of them.

The short service could have served as a prototype for funerals anywhere – a plea to the Almighty to change his mind, forgive and forget and let the deceased through the pearly gates. However, Duncan Cameron had never been a favourite with the minister, who anyway was still smarting from the sentiments that Cameron had managed to get across during their final interview. The minister, therefore, while prepared to make allowances for a mind clouded by haemorrhage and to intercede on his behalf with God, found himself unable to find anything suitably flattering to say about the dead man and it was left to Stuart to utter a few words of eulogy. This he managed by leaning heavily on the loving care that his uncle had lavished on an orphan boy and the wise counsel that he had given him over the years. He skidded lightly, as if on thin ice, over the years during which his uncle's nature had changed and he, Stuart, had allowed himself to be dominated rather than endure a confrontation. The general feeling seemed to be that he had done the best that could be expected with the material available to him.

Funerals are notorious for attracting appropriate weather. Rain had returned, light but colder as autumn approached. Most of the mourners, having once paid their respects, could be expected to make for their cars rather than face the graveside. Grace did the same, leaving Stuart, supporting himself on one stick, to shake the multitude of proffered hands and mention that there would be refreshments available in the nearby Morangie Hotel. To the closer of friends or relations, he whispered an invitation to lunch in the hotel.

Grace sat in Stuart's car, looking towards the graveyard and vaguely looking forward to the end of another awful day and a new beginning to life, not as guests in her parents' house but in their own home.

A car pulled up nearby, seeking but not finding a parking space at the roadside and coming to rest where any traffic would have to take turns in filtering past. Three men got out. They wore dark raincoats so she thought at first that they were mourners who had arrived late. But their behaviour caught her attention and held it. One of the men circled around the mourners, inconspicuously taking photographs with a small camera. A second stood watching dispassionately. The third spoke to the two sextons who were standing by to fill the grave. The sextons slipped quietly away.

The stalwarts who had attended the graveside trickled towards the cars. Stuart followed, limping and using his stick. A large, black van was reversing towards the further gateway. The man who had spoken to the sextons was having a word with the minister, who was looking in Stuart's direction. The man was the taller of the two by half a head.

Grace quitted the car in a hurry and met Stuart. 'There's something wrong,' she said. She eased him round and took his other arm as they walked back.

'What could possibly be wrong?' Stuart asked. 'It all seemed to go quite smoothly.'

'Perhaps I'm mistaken. I hope I am. But those men seemed to

be telling the sextons not to fill in the grave. Let's just find out who they are and what they're up to.'

'I still don't see what could be wrong,' Stuart said. He seemed only half convinced by her qualms but Grace could feel a slight tension in his arm.

The tall man left the minister and came to meet them. 'You're Mr Campbell? The next of kin?'

'I am.'

'Detective Inspector Fauldhouse. I have to tell you that a question has been raised regarding the conduct of Mr Cameron's affairs during the last part of his life. A death certificate was issued but the Procurator Fiscal has ordered the body to be removed for post mortem examination.'

In the silence that followed, Grace thought that she could not only hear her own heartbeat but Stuart's also. Her mind wanted to wander off into some cosier pasture but she forced herself to pay attention. The policeman's manner was mildly apologetic but firm. He was no broader than the average so that his height made him look deceptively thin. He was in middle age but he still had most of his grizzled hair, trimmed short. He had what Grace could only think of as a 'respectable' face, a face that would have looked well on a town clerk or a bank manager, with neat features and a very tidy moustache. The chill breeze seemed to be troubling him. Feeling that he had shown enough respect to the dead, he replaced the hat that he had been carrying, completing the picture of the reputable man in a boring job.

'Can you just do that?' Grace asked. 'Don't you need an exhumation order or something?'

DI Fauldhouse looked at her without emotion. 'The burial was not completed, so this isn't an exhumation. The Procurator Fiscal can call for an autopsy in any case where suspicions have been aroused.'

'Suspicions?' said Stuart. 'What suspicions?' He sounded querulous. Grace knew exactly how he felt. A bad day was heading into disaster.

The Detective Inspector paused, considering. 'It may well be that there is nothing wrong about the death of Mr Cameron. I'm sure I hope so, for your sakes. But even if the death was exactly as certified, there will remain the matter that aroused suspicions in the first place. That will have to be investigated and you will certainly have to know about it, so I see no harm in telling you this much.

'Mr Cameron named as his executor Mr Isaacson, the manager of the Inverness branch of the Caledonian Building Society. When Mr Isaacson visited you to collect the will, he was told that Mr Cameron had been incapacitated for a matter of some weeks. But a substantial sum had been withdrawn from his account with the Building Society during the period between the time of his stroke and his death. Do you know whether Mr Cameron authorised anyone to make a withdrawal from his account?'

'No,' Stuart said slowly. 'I'm absolutely sure that he didn't.'

'Then you will no doubt be seeing me again. Good day to you.'

Having dropped his bombshell, the Detective Inspector strode back to his car, which had moved away to let the mourners drive off but had now returned. He was driven away, leaving his two colleagues to supervise the raising of the coffin and its transfer to the mortuary van. Presumably they were to accompany the body to wherever it was going. The undertaker's men were left to tidy the flowers around the empty grave.

Stuart and Grace looked at each other is stunned silence. 'Smile,' Stuart said at last. 'We've just got to be on *Candid Camera.*'

'I don't quite believe this either,' Grace said. 'I hate death. I don't like the idea of burial. But an autopsy – that's the worst of all.'

Stuart was holding her arm for his own support as they walked. Grace squeezed his hand and received an answering pressure.

In the car and heading for the Morangie Hotel, they arrived at the obvious agreement. The news of the missing money would become public property within a day or two. But by then Duncan Cameron's death would probably have been confirmed as natural. An explanation for the withdrawal of the money might have been found and the culprit, if there was a culprit, arrested. Until that day, there was nothing to be gained by setting off endless speculation and suspicion.

So Grace and Stuart followed their guests to the hotel and went to play host and hostess, distributing beer and spirits to the guests and then providing lunch for the very much smaller number of closer friends and family. The latter was represented by two cousins at least as old as the deceased, who hated each other but had never been known to miss the chance of a free drink or a meal. Grace noticed that each guest struggled to find one compliment to pay to the deceased and then settled in relief to talk about something else.

If any of the guests had noticed anything amiss at the funeral, they had more tact than to say so. But the talk would begin soon enough. Grace smiled and nodded as she was told, for the umpteenth time, what a charmer Stuart's uncle had been in his younger days. Her face was beginning to ache.

Chapter Six

Somehow they managed to endure as that terrible day ground onward. They exchanged banalities with comparative strangers without afterwards remembering a single word, struggling always to appear no more upset than was to be expected after a death in the family. They grappled the secret to themselves, longing for the comfort of diluting it by sharing it with others but knowing too well the scandal that might follow. The scandal might prove to be inevitable but, as they had agreed, there was always the chance that by the time the news escaped, the death would have been found natural and the thief caught. They escaped from the lunch, Stuart wrote a cheque for the uncomfortably large bill and they fled for home.

Stuart was still not ready to drive. As they turned onto the main road, his hand went to his pocket and he hesitated. He had almost stopped smoking and never smoked indoors, but this was a day when any small comfort might help and the weather would not suit his usual outdoor seat. Grace saw the small movement in the corner of her eye and she softened. 'Go ahead,' she said gently. 'Smoke if you want to. Just open a window first.' She disapproved of smoking on professional grounds and she wanted Stuart to live forever; but Stuart's uncle had been rabidly antismoking and had tried, with some success, to forbid it even in Stuart's own house. Perversely, Grace took this to mean that smoking might not be so bad after all. She could have welcomed the comfort that it seemed to give but she hated the taste.

They were still sleeping at the Gillespie's house in Dornoch, but they were on the point of moving and for the moment Strathmore seemed the place to be. When they came to the roundabout, Grace turned the car in that direction, along the south side of the Firth.

Stuart opened his window. He tried to puff his smoke out of the narrow slit. 'This is not going to be good,' he said at last.

'No,' Grace said. She lowered her window a few inches. It produced a gale of wind across the car but they had both come to accept this. Grace turned up the heater to offset the cold. 'It's not going to be good. Stuart, I've never asked you this, but how did your uncle leave his money?'

She saw the hand in her vision make a disclaiming gesture. 'I haven't the faintest idea. We never discussed it and the will was sealed in an envelope with "My will – deliver to Mr Isaacson" written on it. Frankly, I never thought that he had anything worth leaving. He gave the impression that he only had his pensions and maybe a small annuity. I never asked him to contribute to the housekeeping and he hardly ever offered. That was all right. After all, he was functioning as an unpaid housekeeper and he cost me very little beyond his food.'

'I can't see the police getting so steamed up if he only had peanuts to leave.'

'I don't know about that,' Stuart said thoughtfully. 'Suppose he had fifty quid in the building society. That's small enough change, these days. Then it turns out that that fifty quid was drawn out while he was incapacitated and just before his death. They'd have to look into it and at the same time they'd have to take a good, hard look at the death. People have been killed for less. And people have been killed when somebody only *thought* that there was money tucked away or that they stood to benefit in some other way. People have been killed out of hatred or envy or just to shut them up.'

'All right, I'll watch my mouth.'

Stuart managed a laugh of sorts. 'I didn't mean you. You're unique among women. You never waste a word. You're the least garrulous woman I've ever met.'

'Well, good for me!' The silence lasted for several twisting miles until Grace broke it again. 'I can't begin to believe that he was killed,' she said at last. 'It seemed a typical death of a stroke patient. Even the doctor was satisfied. But theft, yes, that happens. Dozens of people were in and out of his room since his stroke. Friends. Us. Nurses. The doctor. The minister. Ambulance men.'

'Policemen,' said Stuart.

'Those too. Any of them could have pinched his building society book. Is that what they'd have had to do?'

'I've no idea.'

They arrived at the place where Grace's own car had been wrecked when she was forced off the road. Instinctively, she slowed. The road was slippery under the thin rain and the place was unlucky for her. 'I think they've got it all wrong,' she said. 'Even if your uncle was killed – which I still don't accept – the two things must be unconnected. After all, if somebody was emptying his building society account, his victim's death would be the one thing most likely to expose the crime. The thief would want him to live on for years, by which time the details would be clouded, records lost, memories dead and nobody to care.'

Stuart tried to tap his ash out of the narrow slit of the window. It blew back over his dark suit. He brushed at it listlessly and then gave up. 'So, unless there's been a startling coincidence, his death was natural?'

'Right.'

'I hope the police see it that way.' After another mile he continued. 'I'm not sure that I go along with that. You can't call something a coincidence if both parts were provoked by the same event. My uncle has a stroke. That gives somebody a chance to rob his building society account. And somebody else, who has something to gain from his death or to fear from his living, thinks, "Here's my chance. If he slips away now, it'll be taken as a natural consequence of the stroke." I'm not saying that that's what happened,' Stuart added quickly. 'Just that if they did both happen, it needn't have been such an amazing coincidence.'

'I think I see what you mean.' Grace gave a deep sigh. 'How long will it be before we can settle down to a normal married life?'

'At the present rate of progress,' Stuart said, 'bloody years.'

They had been driving with the hill rising on their left, grass at first and dotted with cattle, giving way to forestry above and then heather-girt hilltop lost in low cloud. Now they came at last to the cluster of three houses on the right, sandwiched between the road and the flat agricultural land fronting onto Dornoch Firth.

First was George – 'Geordie' – Munro's house, a small bungalow, inherited from their parents, where he lived with his sister.

The house was in need of painting but the garden, largely given over to vegetables, was immaculate. Geordie's dog, Maisie, lay outside the front door, watching for intruders with a jaundiced eye. She would not move until Geordie's return. She was friendly disposed to Grace, but unfortunately this meant that she was jealous of Bonzo – another reason for leaving the puppy in Dornoch for the moment, until time could be spared for formal introductions.

The middle house differed from the other two in having dormer windows to rooms in the roof. It belonged to a couple named Sands who had been out of the country for several years while Henry Sands was on an engineering contract in Africa. The house had been let occasionally on short terms while Geordie Munro had been charged with keeping all in order and the garden tidy. In the latter he had far exceeded his brief and the garden was as perfect as his own and much more floriferous. Henry and Violet Sands, on their return to Scotland at around the time of Duncan Cameron's stroke, had been loud in their surprise and praise. Stuart had known the couple for years, off and on, but Grace had only met them once in passing.

The third house was, of course, Strathmore, a roomy bungalow. Its big back garden would once have put even the other two to shame in tidiness and colour if not in design, but it had been torn apart. Grace glimpsed it between the houses. The earth shaping was finished, the walls and steps were in and brick paving was being laid. A small machine was in use, cultivating and smoothing the site of the future lawn.

Grace slowed again to make the sharp turn into the driveway. 'Hello!' she said. 'That's funny!'

'What is?' Stuart sounded alarmed. The day's events had set his nerves on edge.

'This is refuse day. I left the wheelie-bin out and Geordie did the same. Geordie and Hilda can't be back yet because they have to wait for Alicia; and her Ka was still in the park when we left. I think Henry and Violet are away again. But the bins have vanished. I was just reminding myself to take ours in, so I noticed straight away.' Grace pulled up outside the garage beside the van used by the landscaping foreman. 'And I think I see the culprit. Remember him?'

'Reluctantly, yes.'

'I didn't recognise him earlier, out of context, but he was one of the three policemen at the funeral.' Grace got out of the car. 'Sergeant Ballintore.'

Detective Sergeant Ballintore was arriving in the driveway from behind the house. He represented the whole of the CID based in Dornoch. He lifted a forefinger in a half-salute. 'Miss Gillespie. Mrs Campbell, I should say. And Mr Campbell. This is a bad business. Not the way you would want to start your married lives at all.' He circled the car and offered Stuart a hand to get up to his feet.

Stuart accepted the pull and rose to his full height. Grace handed him his stick. 'I take it that you're responsible for moving the wheelie-bins?'

The Sergeant looked embarrassed. 'Useful information often gets thrown out with the rubbish,' he said. 'It's routine to examine the bins. I put them round the back until the bin-lorry has gone by. We won't take them away,' he added in reassurance. 'Somebody will be back with my car and some bags shortly.'

'That's all very well,' Stuart said. 'But we have some experience of being investigated.'

'You were never suspect,' the Sergeant said quickly.

'And we are suspects this time?'

The Sergeant bridled. 'I did not say that. Mr Campbell, you must see our position. We are informed that money has gone missing and the victim died suddenly, immediately afterwards. It is in your own interests that our investigation be as thorough as possible.'

'That does seem fair,' Grace told Stuart.

'So was my question,' Stuart said grimly.

'It is much too early to have suspects,' said the Sergeant. Perhaps to make up for his scrutiny on a previous occasion, he seemed to be going out of his was to be pacific. 'Once we have investigated, we may have suspects; and I hope that you will not be on that list. It is just unfortunate that you have to be inconvenienced. Your house and possessions will have to be searched. There are SOCOs on the way.'

'Scene Of Crime Officers?' Grace said incredulously. 'But this isn't a crime scene.'

'If there was a crime, here is where it must have been committed,' Sergeant Ballintore pointed out. 'Whether we mean your uncle's death or the theft of his building society card, it happened here. It will be anyone's guess how much time they will need. You may go to a hotel if you so wish, but I suggest that Mrs Gillespie would still be happy to accommodate you. My instructions are to take you inside, one by one, to collect any of your immediate needs. After that, I am to keep the keys. Your car will have to stay here. Transport will be provided to take you to where you intend to stay.'

'And will transport be provided to take me to my school every day? I'll remind you that I'm a depute headmaster and that term begins shortly. If I have to take a taxi, who pays?'

'I will see to it that your car is searched and cleared as soon as possible. Now...?' Detective Sergeant Ballintore turned invitingly towards the house.

'Hold on a minute,' Grace said. 'Almost the only fact that Mr Fauldhouse gave us was that there had been some withdrawals from Mr Cameron's account. What are we talking about here? A large sum or a small one? How was it drawn out? Do you have a description?'

Before deciding that it would be in order to answer the question, the Sergeant seemed to consult some inner oracle. 'I believe that it was drawn out in cash,' he said at last, 'from the ATM in Dornoch or one in Tain, at the maximum of two hundred and fifty pounds a day for a period of several weeks. The withdrawals were made after night fell. We do not have a picture by CCTV. And that is all I know.'

'I never knew that he had that sort of money.' Stuart's jaw was beginning to jut. 'So, what if we decide that we won't let you bugger up our lives because of what may very well turn out to be a peculation or a clerical error or computer fraud in the building society's office?'

'Then you will force us to obtain a search warrant to which you can, of course, object through your solicitor.' The Sergeant sounded genuinely apologetic.

'I think,' Grace said, 'that we may get our house back quicker if we let the police get on with it.' (The Sergeant was nodding.) 'But we'll have to get into the house to phone my mother. We'd planned to eat here this evening. Sensible people don't take mobile phones to a funeral in case they start ringing in the middle of the service.'

The Sergeant produced a mobile phone.

'You get back in the car for the moment,' Grace told her husband. 'I'll do what's needed. Tell me what else you want from here. He is still not fit to stand for long in a cold wind,' she added to the Sergeant. 'And then we might have a word with the gardeners.'

DS Ballintore hesitated as though wondering whether Stuart might tamper with evidence in the car. Evidently he decided that Stuart was unlikely to sin, or else that any evidence was unlikely to be in the car, bearing in mind that any evildoing had been in the house. 'That will be quite all right,' he said.

'I should think so,' Grace said. She phoned her mother, avoiding for the moment any mention of theft or suspicion, and returned the phone to the Sergeant.

When she went to help Stuart out of the car, he shook his head. 'I don't think I could work up a head of steam about the garden just now,' he said.

Grace pursed her lips. 'I for one do not intend to let the police, a thief or even a murderer prevent my life going forward as much as it still can. I'm going to look round the garden,' she said.

'You're right,' Stuart said. He sounded mildly surprised. He held out his hand for Grace to give him a helpful pull.

Chapter Seven

Events of such moment could never have remained secret for long. Word had begun to circulate in the area, emanating either from the sextons or from those among the last mourners to leave the graveside who had seen the filling in of the grave stopped. Mr Gillespie heard whispers among the business community and communicated them to his wife. That evening, at the Gillespie family home in Dornoch, there was much agitated speculation although, for lack of almost anything resembling a concrete fact, only the vaguest hypotheses were possible. Anyone telephoning for news was told the truth – that the Campbells had been told almost nothing.

That particular truth did not prevent discussion throughout the evening meal and it continued after they had transferred into the pleasantly old fashioned sitting room. The general consensus was that Duncan Cameron's death had been perfectly natural – a second stroke brought on by his fury at learning that his lovingly tended garden was being torn apart.

The theft of money from his building society account was different. A dozen people had been in and out of the sickroom. 'When I came back to Strathmore after his stroke, I saw something that I seem to remember looked like what I imagine a building society card looks like,' Grace said. She paused, wondering whether to reword the sentence and then decided that they probably knew what she meant. 'There were some pieces of paper under it. He probably kept his PIN number written down.'

'He did,' Stuart said.

'I thought as much,' Grace said. 'Not many elderly people trust themselves to remember numbers. I was looking in a top drawer of his chest of drawers for a clean handkerchief for him – he hated using tissues – and that's when I saw whatever I saw.'

'But did you see it again after we came back?' Stuart asked.

'I don't remember seeing it. But then, I don't remember not seeing it,' Grace told him. 'I don't think I had occasion to go to the drawer again. Could somebody draw money out of somebody else's account without the book?'

'It depends on the kind of account,' said her mother. 'I kept my little savings in the building society at one time. Some accounts are operated by a card and a PIN number, just like your account at the bank.'

'I don't know anything about the system,' Stuart said, 'but I can tell you this. If they had the card or the book, they'd have the PIN number. My uncle had a current account with a local bank and he forgot his PIN number once and had to borrow from me until they furnished a new one. The hurt to his pride rankled. After that, he wrote his PIN number in his chequebook. I begged him not to, but he always knew best. It's a safe assumption that he wrote any PIN number down somewhere, just as Grace said. He may – or may not – have had the sense to juggle the figures a bit, but any half-intelligent crook would soon puzzle it out.'

They could get no further that evening, but next morning they were provided with more facts than they cared to handle.

Detective Inspector Fauldhouse arrived before the breakfast dishes had been cleared away. He was accompanied by Detective Sergeant Ballintore and a constable who was well provided with notebooks and tape recorders. Grace took the policemen into her mother's sitting room, where Stuart was already waiting in one of the armchairs with his feet on a stool.

'I would like to see you one at a time,' said the DI.

'No,' said Stuart. He was regarded with surprise by the whole company – Grace because, out of school, authoritativeness was not in Stuart's nature and the others because the police are not accustomed to being spoken to by the public in a manner both firm and polite but negative.

'Why not?' Fauldhouse enquired coldly.

'My wife and I,' Stuart said, 'have shared the same experiences. We have the same evidence to give. The fact that you want to see us separately suggests that you hope to trap us into contradicting each other. You're getting this down?' he asked the constable, who had seated himself at a corner table.

The constable looked up from his notebook and nodded. 'Yes.'

'Very well. That in turn suggests that you suspect one or both of us of something, in which case we will only be interviewed separately if our solicitor is present.'

'The reason that we want to see you separately is so that you will not colour each other's recollections,' said the DI.

'That sounds very reasonable but we are more likely to refresh each other's memories.'

DI Fauldhouse thought for a few seconds. His face gave nothing away. 'Very well,' he said at last. 'We shall see.' For the written record and for the benefit of the tape recorder, he took pains to get the spelling of their names and address correct.

'That deals with us,' Stuart said. 'Now let's talk about you. Are you in charge of this case?'

The DI seemed to think the question a reasonable one. 'For the moment,' he said, 'yes. If the autopsy finds anything irregular in your uncle's death, I would expect to continue but probably under the supervision of a more senior officer. That, I may say, would be very unlikely to be Superintendent Largs, since you're both acquainted with him and his wife. I'm under instructions to treat you no differently from how I would treat any member of the public without senior friends on the Force.'

'We wouldn't expect any special treatment,' Stuart said. 'All right. Fire away.'

The DI nodded. 'Yesterday, I informed you that your uncle's building society account had been very largely emptied.'

'I knew that he had a current account at the bank,' Stuart said. 'He gave me a small cheque towards his share of the household bills whenever he felt rich, which was not very often. Or, in view of what I've been told, perhaps I should have said, "whenever he admitted to feeling rich". I told him not to bother, more fool me, but now and again he would insist and I let him keep his pride. I didn't even know that he had an account with a building society.'

DI Fauldhouse switched his look of enquiry to Grace, who said, 'I suspected that he had an account because I saw what looked like a building society card once in his drawer when I was getting him a clean handkerchief. It didn't really register at the time, but it lingered in my subconscious memory because the design was familiar. I had a patient, about two years ago, who had an account with the same building society and he used to get me to draw money for him. He gave me his PIN number. Some people trust me, Inspector. I got a Christmas card from him, last year, and some flowers by Interflora.'

The Inspector looked at Grace for a moment but decided not to pursue that side issue. 'Did you happen to notice the amount to Mr Cameron's credit?' he asked

'I didn't see a book, only a card, rather like a credit card or a bank card. Are we allowed to know how much has gone missing?'

'A substantial sum. That's all that I'm prepared to say at the moment. Did you touch the card?'

'I don't think so, unless my fingers brushed it as I reached for a handkerchief.'

'How often did you go to that drawer?'

Grace bridled. 'Only once. I thought I'd told you that. Trying to catch me out, Inspector?'

Detective Inspector Fauldhouse met Grace's eye blandly but she sensed that he was secretly amused. 'No, Mrs Campbell, I am not trying to catch you out. What you said was that you saw the card only once. Correct, Constable?'

'Correct, Sir.'

'What I'm trying to get at, Mrs Campbell, is whether you ever had occasion to look in that drawer again and the card was not there at that time.'

Grace felt her face grow hot. 'Inspector, I apologise. But so far as I remember, I never had occasion to go to that drawer except once. I came here to nurse Stuart and give him physiotherapy and at that time his uncle was in perfect health and rather hostile. I would never have ventured into his room. After he had his stroke, he was removed to Raigmore, in Inverness. He was only brought back here after we had left for our honeymoon. He then had two nurses to look after him. We had only been home for a very few days, and staying with my mother, when he died.'

'But presumably his used handkerchiefs were laundered. Who put them back in the drawer?'

Grace thought hard. 'I've no idea,' she said at last. 'I don't remember ever doing it. Hilda Munro did his laundry to help the nurses, but as to whether she or they put the laundered hankies back in his drawer, you'd have to ask them.'

The Inspector returned his attention to Stuart. 'On that subject, Mr Campbell, have you anything to add?'

'Not a thing.'

'Do you know the contents of your uncle's will?'

Stuart shook his head. 'No. I knew that he'd made a will, because he left instructions that it should be delivered to Mr Isaacson. And I knew that Mr Isaacson was a building society manager, because it said so on the envelope, but I never even thought about a connection. I wasn't interested in how he had left his money because I never thought that the old chap had anything worth leaving. He had an insurance policy to cover funeral expenses, because he told me so. And that's all that I ever knew about his finances. He sometimes made a modest contribution to household expenses and I assumed that that was all he could afford. It seems that I may have been wrong.'

Stuart paused and waited, but the Inspector seemed engrossed in watching the Constable's pen making squiggles across the page. 'How much money was withdrawn?' Stuart asked.

'I'm waiting for confirmation of the figure but I can assure you that it runs to several thousand pounds.'

'I'm amazed that he had that much. Is there any indication as to where it came from?'

'I was about to ask you the same question. It seems to have been paid in to the account in Inverness, in cash, in several instalments, since his retirement. We shall certainly be trying to trace its origins. Your uncle was in the navy?'

'He retired as a chief petty officer,' Stuart said.

'Not savings from his pay,' said the Chief Inspector thoughtfully.

'Gambling wins, perhaps,' Grace said firmly.

DI Fauldhouse raised his eyebrows. 'Was your uncle a gambler?' he asked Stuart

'Not that I was aware of. He would never have admitted any such thing to me. But I suppose he might have had a share in a pools syndicate in one of his clubs. Or premium bonds or the lottery.'

'From what we've heard of him so far, he was the sort of man who would consider gambling to be a deadly sin.'

'That was true in recent years. He was a bit of a lad in his youth, so I'm told,' Stuart said.

'But after his retirement?'

Nobody commented. Duncan Cameron's strict code in later life was too well known to require it.

'When is the autopsy to take place?' Stuart asked suddenly to break the silence.

'It's happening now,' said the Inspector.

'Then we'll know soon, one way or the other?'

'I wouldn't hold your breath,' said Sergeant Ballintore, opening his mouth for the first time since his arrival. The Inspector frowned at the informality while nodding agreement.

'I don't understand,' Stuart said.

'Then I'll take it on myself to explain it to you,' Grace said wearily. 'I've seen it all before. I was nursing a lottery winner after a car smash. He seemed to be making a full recovery but suddenly he collapsed and died. His widow was a biochemist with a roving eye, so they gave it the full treatment. The pathologist rather fancied me, I think, and he told me quite a lot about what went on.

'An autopsy looking for injury or disease needn't take so long. The signs are there to be seen. But when there's a possibility of poison being used, it's what they call a whole new ballgame. Of all the chemical compounds in the world, about a hundred thousand are in daily use in industry, agriculture or medicine. Some are more poisonous than others, depending on the dosage, but almost anything is a poison if you take enough of it. Not one of them is wholly undetectable, but some of them may have effects that will be concealed or duplicated by the first stages of decomposition.'

'In other words,' Stuart said, 'it can take time.'

'And a lot of it,' said Grace. 'Especially if the pathologist didn't get to the body immediately. I'm sorry, Stuart,' she added, 'I know we're talking about your uncle, but you did ask. Laboratory instruments have produced a lot of short cuts but it can still come down to trial and error, such as giving samples to laboratory animals and waiting to see what happens. Your uncle was on quite a lot of medication, which may make it even more difficult, because I suppose they'll have to determine what sort of doses he seems to have been given. Well, if they find any traces of poisons or lethal doses of medication, no doubt the Inspector will tell us.'

Detective Inspector Fauldhouse smiled without humour. 'Believe me,' he said, 'you may well be the first to know.' He hesitated but curiosity overcame his reserve. 'I remember the case you mentioned but I never heard the outcome.'

'There hasn't been what you'd call an outcome,' said Grace. 'They managed to prove poisoning by insulin, but they never had a strong enough case against the wife or anybody else. She's still at liberty and she married again. She married a colleague at the laboratory where she worked.'

'One last question. There was a photograph in a frame. It seems old. Who would that have been?'

'We don't know either,' Stuart said.

'Indeed? When we removed it from the frame there was one word written on the back. Love. Just that and no more.'

'I can only suppose,' said Stuart, 'that he must have had a romance in his life that I knew nothing about. When do we get back into our house?'

'The SOCOs will need most of tomorrow. After all,' the Inspector said reasonably, 'now that suspicions have been aroused we can hardly leave the guilty party to tamper with any evidence that may have been left behind.'

'I suppose not,' said Stuart. 'All right, do your damnedest, Inspector, but do it as quickly as you can.'

They were left in limbo for more than another day. To keep her mind from tracing every possible permutation of events past and to come, Grace played with Bonzo and continued the elementary processes of training. They began to form a bond. Stuart had no concentration to spare for any sensible activity. He might have filled the time with a visit to his school, but his car had not yet been released and Mr Gillespie's car was in use for most of each day. Grace kept up her own exercise regime and put extra time into Stuart's recovery, working his joints and massaging his muscles until he swore that enough was enough. 'The French say that better is the enemy of good,' he told her.

'The French talk a lot of rubbish. And it's high time that you were exercising yourself instead of expecting me to do your work for you.'

The two nurses, they heard, had been given beds at the Munros' house. Grace met Alicia in a Dornoch shop. The nurse was reserved but Grace persuaded her to share coffee in the Castle Hotel. When they were alone in the upstairs lounge, Grace said, 'You must be getting as much hassle as we are. I'm sorry that you've been dragged into this.'

The nurse shrugged. 'Worse for you,' she said in her warm Caribbean tones. 'We can take it. Miss Munro's all steamed up. They've been asking her if she saw the old man's cashcard in the drawer when she put his handkerchiefs back and did she notice any numbers written on a piece of paper at the time. And they've been prying into how much money she has – she has an account in the same building society.'

'I suppose she blames us?'

Alicia's eyes shone in her dark face. 'She doesn't know who to blame so she blames everybody. It's not a comfortable house to stay in, just now.'

'I'll keep out of her way for a while,' Grace said. 'Tell me, while we were away and up to the time he died, who could have taken the card out of the drawer.'

'The world and his wife,' said Alicia. 'We've tried to list them for the bluebottles, but we may have left half of them out. Members of his church and clubs felt obliged to call. I don't remember any of them calling twice,' she added.

'I suppose not. I wouldn't have, myself.'

It was the Thursday afternoon before Stuart began to lose patience. Without access to a car, the school would only have been accessible to him by the bus, which ran infrequently and at impossible times, or by taxi for which he had no intention of paying. In any case the preparations for the coming term were almost complete and even in his absence could be expected to roll towards completion under their own momentum. All his personal chattels were at Strathmore. He was still not recovered enough to walk more than a limited distance for recreation. He had already read most of the books in the house. He was reduced to sitting in the garden or watching daytime television. He wondered which bored him more.

In desperation, he began phoning the police, demanding to know when he and Grace might return to their home. None of the appropriate officers seemed to be available but eventually he got a message, relayed from DI Fauldhouse, the burden of which was 'Not yet'.

Grace was becoming just as impatient. Without the tools of her physiotherapy, her treatment of Stuart's lingering injuries was limited. She was also eager to begin married life in her own home, now that it was relieved of the wearisome presence of Stuart's uncle. Late that afternoon, she borrowed her father's car and chauffeured Stuart the half-hour's drive to Strathmore. The area of tarmac was generous but it was partly occupied by a van from the landscaping firm and another that was unmarked but in the blue and white colours favoured by the police. The skip loaded with the plants removed from the garden took up some more space. Grace squeezed the car onto the last vacant strip and partly on the grass. A local policeman politely and apologetically but firmly barred them from entry, but through a window they glimpsed a figure in white overalls performing some unidentifiable task.

The constable had been at school with Grace, though some

years her junior, and he had been a pupil under Stuart. He was properly respectful but though the couple occupied the moral high ground he could not disobey his masters. His orders were to prevent unauthorised entry until the Forensic staff had given the all clear and to see that the house was properly locked and sealed when left empty. His orders, he said, had not included anything about the garden, so they made their way round the house.

It was a bare and desolate scene, but the foreman from the landscaping firm was still there, attending to some details and removing tools to his van. He was a thickset man with dark hair and blue stubble showing on his hollow cheeks. May Largs had introduced him as Mr Hodges. Outside the range of his hearing, she said that he had seldom been known to smile, but that was probably because he was not prepared to stand any nonsense from the plants or the people associated with them. She added that on no account must they lend him any money, no matter how plausible the story, because he was a compulsive gambler. Grace had nursed the brother of one gambling man and knew only too well that the chance of any such loan being repaid was negligible.

The sunshine had made a return but it could do little to brighten up a scene of creative devastation. It was soon clear that to Mr Hodges the site was far from barren but that the spindly plants that lurked insignificantly between stretches of the dark brown peat were already stretching upward and, in his mind, bursting into full bloom. 'If this weather holds,' he said, 'you should have grass showing by this time next week. Remember, you give it the first cut with nail scissors.'

The joke, modest though it was, came as a welcome surprise to Grace after the anxious and dreary days that had passed and coming from the usually saturnine Mr Hodges. All the same, she felt that as the employer and as a woman the last word was her prerogative. 'I'll remember,' she said, dead-pan. 'But your quotation included for giving the grass its first cut. I'll come back and remind you. I'll even bring the nail scissors.'

Mr Hodges looked at her sharply and realised that she had produced a riposte to his humour. He almost smiled and then became serious again. 'That's our work finished,' he said, 'all but raking the peat and planting two trees that were out of stock. It'll look better in the spring with the alpines and rock-plants out, better still the following year when the shrubs are coming on, but you won't see it at its very best until the year after that.'

'And then we'll be due to have it done all over again?' Stuart asked.

Mr Hodges looked shocked. 'Certainly not! All you need do is hoe between the plants if any weeds make it through the peat and cut the grass. Best leave any pruning to us. The next other work you'll need will be to take out a few of the shrubs to make room. Mrs Largs can tell you which, or we can come back and do the work for you.'

'That's fine,' said Grace. 'I think it's all going to look great and be much less work, as it'll need to be now that we don't have Mr Cameron to spend all his time on it.'

They were walking slowly back towards the vehicles. Mr Hodges followed, wheeling the last remaining barrow. 'He had green fingers, did old Mr Cameron,' he said. To Grace, it seemed to be as good an epitaph as the old gent had any right to expect. 'I met him once or twice at the garden centre. Not to say that I knew him, or I would surely have come to see him off at the burying.' Grace stopped to read the label on a shrub and Mr Hodges had to wait. 'But you'll have had plenty folk at the funeral,' he said.

'Plenty,' Stuart agreed. 'Many more than I expected.'

They moved on again.

'It's a nice house you have here,' said Mr Hodges gloomily to their backs, 'and a grand outlook. The right sort of garden will just set it off fine. I'm just doing up my auntie's old house for myself, so I was wondering. Who did your kitchen?'

Stuart named a large firm in Dingwall.

'And did they supply what they call the "white goods"? That fancy microwave oven and the washing machine and all like that?'

'No. I took quotes and ended up buying them from the Hydroelectric Board,' said Stuart.

'Them? Cheap they are not,' said Mr Hodges in tones of woe.

'I will maybe get Mairi in the firm's office to try the Internet for me.'

Grace settled Stuart into the car but paused. Mr Hodges was fitting the barrow into the back of his van. 'When do we get rid of this damn skip?' she asked him.

Mr Hodges straightened a back that seemed to be permanently bent in sympathy with his flowers. 'Don't ask me,' he said sourly. 'Ask him.' He jerked a thumb in the direction of the constable.

'I'm sure I can't tell you, Mrs Campbell.' The constable said. 'Those scientific laddies come and take samples out of it. Mr Fauldhouse says it's not to be taken away until they say so.'

'And a pretty penny it's costing us in rental,' said Mr Hodges. 'The boss will be speaking to Mr Gillespie about it, I've no doubt.'

'Nor have I,' said Grace.

As they crossed the long bridge on the way back to Dornoch, Stuart said, 'It will be all right, won't it? I can't help remembering all the flowers when my uncle was keeping it.'

'All the flowers but none of the shape,' Grace said. 'Of course it'll be all right. Time will come when this is one of our do-you-remembers. We're just depressed, with losing your uncle and then all this fuss and mystery, so it feels as though we'll be stuck with that desolation for years and years. It will all blow past and soon we'll have a lovely garden, I promise you.' As she spoke, she was wondering which of them she was trying to convince. The longer they were kept at bay from their true home, the more the *status quo* seemed to set into a permanency. 'There was about a ton of bulbs and tubers dug in under the ground cover, so you should have plenty of flowers to sit among in the spring.'

'As if I ever had time to sit around!'

'From now on, you have time,' Grace said. Of that, she was determined.

'I don't even *like* sitting around.'

'You do. You just *think* you don't.'

'I have a very low threshold of boredom.' Stuart was beginning to sound sulky.

'You don't have to if you don't want to.'

'Are you humouring me?'

'Of course I am. Isn't that what wives are supposed to do?'

Stuart's grim expression began to soften. 'It's what they're supposed to do, but they don't all do it.'

'That's them. This is me. If I take on a job, I do it. You should know that by now.'

'I do,' Stuart said. He sounded much happier. He put an arm around his wife's waist and squeezed. Grace had done sterling work on those arms and the pressure made both breathing and driving difficult, but she had no intention of asking him to stop. 'You are the queen of wives. You are perfection and I only have a vague idea of what I did to deserve somebody like you.' He recovered his arm and ran his hand up her leg, under her skirt.

'I love it,' Grace said, 'but I don't think that you should do that while I'm driving the car.'

'We could die together. The idea doesn't attract you?'

'Not a lot, I'd prefer that we lived together.'

Stuart made no reply but by moving her head Grace could glimpse him in the driving mirror. He was definitely almost smiling.

Chapter Nine

The officers involved in the case might be grudging with their news, but information did begin to trickle through a less official channel.

Several years earlier, Grace's father had been persuaded, with some difficulty, to have his garden made over to May Largs's design. He had soon come round to the view that the improved appearance and reduced demands on his time had been well worth the cost and this was what had led him to the inspired decision over his daughter's wedding present. It was May's habit to pay occasional visits to "her" gardens, not on a fee basis but just to satisfy herself that her brain-children were in good heart and being accorded the occasional moments of skilled and loving care that she felt they deserved. She arrived the following morning and walked around with Mr Gillespie, but it was evident that her mind was not on the subjects of pruning or thinning-out. Even the emotive subject of couch-grass provoked no more than a passing allusion to touch-tipping.

She soon made an excuse to isolate Grace in the sitting room. The work at Strathmore had been satisfactory – all but the two missing trees – and that topic was very soon dismissed. May leaned closer confidentially. 'I shouldn't be telling you anything,' she said. 'I'm breaking all the rules. But I thought you ought to know what's afoot.'

May felt a flutter in her stomach. 'If Will's been speaking out, for God's sake tell us,' she said. Her breath seemed to be squeezed out of her by the weight of worry. 'We're being kept in the dark and it's driving us mad.'

'That's routine procedure. It doesn't mean a thing. And Will didn't exactly speak out. Husbands aren't as good at keeping secrets as they think they are.'

'Ve haf vays of making you talk?'

May smiled but it was fleeting. 'Not quite that,' she said seriously. 'Because we know you, Will's supposed to stay out of the case except in a purely supervisory sort of way, but he was asked to get some advice from me and I measured out my advice in proportion to the answers I got. I was asked to list the plants that came out of your garden when we cleared it.'

Grace's mind had been running on far different lines. What May had said conveyed no meaning. 'Whatever for?' she asked.

May snapped her fingers. 'Wake up, Grace! Stuart's uncle died suddenly. There was some fiddle in connection with his money and he never was exactly a ray of sunshine. There were no marks or wounds on his body. They wouldn't be doing their jobs if they didn't think about poisons.'

'But the garden?' Grace felt a hollowness in her stomach and her face was prickling as the blood drained away. A vague disquiet that the police were sniffing around had been tolerable and would probably pass. But this was becoming real and menacing.

She was granted a respite as her mother arrived with the inevitable tray of coffee and sweet biscuits. There was an interval of chatter. Mrs Gillespie, it was clear, had mixed emotions. She was torn between regret at the death of Stuart's uncle and indignation at the disturbance to everybody's lives. On the other hand, she was delighted that circumstances had driven her daughter and her new son-in-law back into her clutches, to be nurtured and mollycoddled however she saw fit. The mystery surrounding the death of Stuart's uncle also provided an exciting topic for conversation, but she soon perceived that this was not the moment and she got up to leave. The shops were calling.

As the door closed behind Mrs Gillespie, May said, 'Will thinks they're wasting their time on the garden. There are so many people involved who've been around hospitals. And a lot of people keep lethal drugs tucked away, sleeping tablets and that sort of thing, as a sort of last resort in case of the big C. But you medical people would probably know better than most how to poison somebody with extracts from garden plants and weeds. Have you any idea how many of those are poisonous?'

'There's laburnum,' Grace said haltingly. 'Everybody knows about that. And blue monkshood. And ragwort. And isn't cow parsley...?'

May waved aside Grace's tentative effort. 'I'm always warning people about letting their children browse in the garden. I counted up. Leaving out the ones the books only call *somewhat* poisonous and also the ones that are only skin or eye irritants, I made it seventy-one. Of course, you didn't have all of those in the garden at Strathmore. Only half a dozen or so. And ragwort wasn't on my list. I think it gives horses liver damage but it isn't very harmful to people. Will may be right and they can discount the garden. Most of the natural poisons produce noticeable symptoms.'

Grace tried to make light of it. 'Well, that should let Stuart out. He's been in a hospital, but only as a patient. And he couldn't get around the garden at all.'

May patted her friend's wrist. 'Grace, I know that you and Stuart are as innocent as babes unborn – or even more so, if what they say about original sin is true. But the police can't afford to be so trusting. I'm afraid you'll have to brace yourselves for being under the microscope for some time yet.'

Within the privacy of her mind, Grace said something very rude indeed. Aloud, she said, 'How long?'

'Nobody could tell you that. I went to a conference with Will recently. Tell the truth, it was at a stately home and I only went along because I wanted to see the garden, but I did attend one or two lectures that interested me and one of them was about toxicology. It was a real eye-opener. It isn't easy to define a poison, because most things are poisonous if you take enough of them while many things are beneficial in small doses and killers in large ones. Of more than five million chemical compounds in the world, about a hundred thousand are used every day in agriculture, industry, domestic or pharmacy.'

'I said something like that to Stuart. That must include one heck of a lot of poisons.'

'It does. Once they've eliminated the common and obvious ones, they have computerised machines now that can carry out a whole series of tests, but it all takes time and costs money.'

'So they can't just tell the forensic scientists, "Test for *everything*",' Grace suggested.

May nodded. 'Will says that that would probably cost ten years' budget. So they have to test for the poisons that produce similar sympton and if those tests turn up blank they have to try again and again, looking for other classes of poison. And then, of course, if they find the least trace of something that might have been used they have to consider whether it arrived in the natural way of things. They have to test for it around the house and work out how much of it would be needed for a fatal dose. I'm not putting it very well, but outside of horticulture I'm no scientist.'

'You're putting it too damn well,' Grace said gloomily. 'And what you're saying is that we won't get back into our house for donkeys' ages.'

'I hope I'm wrong. If you think they're being unreasonable, you could always get your solicitor to hurry them up.'

'That might only make them more certain that we were trying to hide something.' Grace was lost in thought for some seconds. 'The stupid thing,' she said at last, 'is that if they find that Mr Cameron was poisoned, we may get back into our house soon. If they can't find anything, this could go on for ever. So on what am I supposed to pin my hopes?'

'Don't ask me,' said May. 'Perhaps you should hope for somebody to have a rush of conscience and confess. Of course, nutcases make false confessions all the time, so perhaps you should amplify that hope a bit and hope that somebody makes a confession and gets believed.'

When May had departed and Stuart returned from his slow walk down to the shops, Grace fetched him into the sitting room for a conference. Her knees had become weak and breath still seemed to be in short supply.

Stuart at first, while agreeing that they wanted their house back, saw no need to involve a solicitor. 'It all costs money and at this stage he couldn't do anything that we couldn't do for ourselves.'

'He might be able to hurry the police up a bit,' Grace said, mindful of May's words.

Stuart's experience with the law had left him less sanguine. 'But who would hurry the solicitor?' he asked. 'I'd like to get back home, but I think we can only wait patiently.'

'You may be right. It happens sometimes – you being right, I mean. But I think we need somebody looking after our interests. Think about it. They suspect poison. Who are they going to suspect? Who might be thought to have the strongest motives? One way of looking at the two happenings together – the death and the robberies – might be to consider that his heirs might have realised that his account was being emptied and, not knowing who was doing it, gave him a nudge quickly while there was still something left. And who might have access to poisons?'

'I see what you mean.' Stuart thought seriously while Grace tried not to look out of the window. The late flowers, mostly roses, only reminded her of the poisons that they might be nurturing. 'I think that it may be your turn to be right,' Stuart said at last.

The premier local solicitor was Andrew McCormick in Tain. He had acted for the Gillespie family in the past and had handled the conveyance of Stuart's house. One phonecall was enough to establish that he was in his office and could make time for them provided that they came immediately.

Mr Gillespie's car was available, for a limited period. Within twenty minutes they tucked into a parking place near the solicitor's office. It was only a short walk and Stuart's knees were working better with each day. Mr McCormick was waiting for them. He was a lean man, well into middle age although he had kept most of his dark hair. His air of quiet confidence helped Grace to subdue her fears. He had once been commissioned in the Highland Regiment, but he never referred to his old rank and a gentle sense of humour relieved his stiffly military bearing. His office, in an old house just off the main road, was approached through an overgrown garden. It was nevertheless surprisingly clean and streamlined, given to electronic aids rather than dusty books.

'I can't say that I'm surprised to see you here,' he said when they were seated. 'I couldn't make it to Mr Cameron's funeral – I sent flowers – but I've been aware of the police interest. In fact, whispers are already going around. Not surprising, bearing in mind that they must be asking some rather pointed questions of many different people. You'd better tell me all about it.'

The story took some time to unfold. They told it in full, by turns, only omitting May's breach of confidentiality. Mr McCormick listened in silence. His hand lay close to the keyboard of a computer – rather, Grace thought, like a cat waiting at a mouse-hole. 'And what brings you here today?' he asked at last.

'They seem to suspect poisoning,' Grace said. 'Isn't that enough?'

'I meant, why today and not yesterday or tomorrow?'

Grace and her husband exchanged a glance. 'I think,' Stuart said, 'that the last straw was the realisation that this could go on for ever if we let it. Assume that my uncle just plain died after somebody looted his building society account. Wrongly associating the two happenings, the police are determined to discover how he was murdered and, if they don't find what doesn't exist, they could go on looking indefinitely.'

'Perhaps it's time for a showdown,' said the solicitor.

Grace was tired of tiptoeing around the subject. 'You mean, tell him to pee or get off the pot,' she said.

Stuart looked shocked but the solicitor only smiled. He began to use the keyboard of his PC. 'I'll try to get hold of DI Fauldhouse. He's not wholly unreasonable. A meeting here or in Dornoch would seem best. You can then be very co-operative until I tell you to stop. When would you be available?'

'Any time,' Stuart said. 'Any time at all.'

Lawyers are not notable for impetuous speed of action, nor are the police famous for hurrying to fit in with the convenience of the public. The Campbells quite expected to have to wait in limbo, at least over the weekend. It came as a surprise when next day, the Saturday, Mr McCormick phoned from his car and then arrived at the Dornoch house in mid-morning.

The Gillespies were out at the time, so the three could settle in the sitting room with no fear of being interrupted with unwanted refreshments.

The solicitor settled his frame into one of the deep chairs and shared a half-smile between his clients. 'After we spoke yesterday, it struck me that there was one area that I could explore that would be relevant. I phoned Dr Sullivan. He had given his patient a full examination not long before the death and he signed the death certificate without reservations, you recall. He was adamant that he saw no prior symptoms and he has already told the police as much – and in no uncertain terms, he assures me. Then I phoned the Detective Inspector. I tried to get him to meet us together. For some reason of his own, he preferred to see me alone and at Strathmore. I met him there an hour ago.'

'Could he not face us?' Grace asked.

'Between ourselves, I think you've put your finger on it. The man is embarrassed. He suspects a particular poison. The toxicologists advise that it is very difficult to detect and they have not yet found any evidence of it. If there had been symptoms prior to the death, they might have been able to make a case, but the doctor will not go along. He told them exactly what he told me – that he examined Mr Cameron just prior to death and there were no discernible symptoms. The Detective Inspector finds himself in an impossible position. He has no grounds for not letting you back into your house but he is concerned in case he allows evidence to be destroyed. Or to look, later, as though it might have been destroyed.'

Grace tried to speak but the solicitor's impassive explanation was lending reality to what had been no more than a fantasy. Her mouth seemed suddenly to have been filled with cotton wool. She looked at her husband. 'What poison?' Stuart asked.

'Ricin.'

'Isn't that the poison that the Bulgarian was killed by in London?' Stuart asked. 'Markov? Injected from a trick umbrella?'

'That's the one,' said the solicitor cheerfully. 'I gather that it's not difficult to acquire. But any fool could make it on the kitchen table, extracting it from *Ricinus Communis*. That's the castor oil plant to you and me. Also known as *Fatsia*.' He produced his modest smile again. 'Forgive me for showing off, but I stopped the car on the way here and checked it out on the Internet.'

The idea of being able to consult the Internet from a car seemed to Grace to be the acme of sophistication but Stuart, who taught physics to teenagers, was of a more technical turn of mind and could readily accept the combination of a laptop computer and a mobile phone. 'I don't suppose I've ever been within a mile of a castor oil plant,' he said.

'I'm afraid that you've been within much less than a mile to one or more,' said Mr McCormick. 'There are several varieties of it, but one of them was present as a great tangle in the skip, awaiting removal. The plant with the thick, shiny, dark green leaves.'

'That horrible thing? For once,' Stuart said, 'my uncle and I were in absolute agreement. An aunt of mine – his sister-in-law – gave him a plant in a pot for his birthday. He said that it was the ugliest brute that he'd ever seen. It's supposed to be an indoor plant, this far north, but he put it out into the garden. The idea was that the frosts would kill it off and he could then tell my aunt quite truthfully that it had died, but we had two very mild winters in a row and the damn thing was romping away, quite out of control. He was going to dig it out and burn it, but then he had his stroke and it was left for the landscaping contractor to dispose of. I never knew what the hell it was and I don't think I ever touched it.'

'Let's hope that the police accept your assurance to that effect. In our favour is the fact that ricin takes on average six to eight hours to kill a person – which would suggest that it had been administered at some time in the small hours of that morning. The symptoms depend on the means of administration, but are of progressive heart failure and a number of other signs of distress that the doctor says were definitely not present when he examined him. He insists, in fact, that the old chap's heart was the best organ he had left.

'That, you'll appreciate, leaves Mr Fauldhouse caught between a rock and a hard place. The Forensic Science section usually lurks in its laboratories, leaving the SOCOs to gather all the evidence and samples under their direction; but now they're on site and going over the house again, looking for signs that the SOCOs may have missed – signs that somebody has been processing castor oil plants to extract ricin. Frankly, I think that the DI would jump at any excuse to accept the death as natural and quite unconnected with the theft from the building society account, but the Procurator Fiscal won't settle for any such simple solution and the doctor won't change his story. So! I'll contact the Inspector, tell him what you've just told me and say that you'll both meet him and sign statements setting out the facts about the castor oil plant and flatly denying everything else. Don't discuss anything else with him unless I'm present.'

Some moisture had returned to Grace's mouth and she had found her voice. 'How far have they got on the stolen money?' she asked.

'Quite a long way. The withdrawals began more than a month ago and a total of fifteen withdrawals were made, each of the maximum of two hundred and fifty pounds. According to my rather shaky mental arithmetic, that adds up to a total of three thousand, seven hundred and fifty pounds. Each withdrawal was made at night from the ATM in Tain or Dornoch.'

Stuart's mouth had fallen open. 'I had no idea that my uncle had that sort of money,' he said at last.

'He had rather more than that sort of money,' Mr McCormick retorted. 'I understand that there remains a matter of eleven thousand in the account.'

'But this is amazing,' said Stuart. 'Do they have any idea where the money came from?'

'Oh yes. An idea. They know the source but not the source of the source, if I may put it that way. The Detective Inspector was quite frank about that.' The solicitor frowned at the ceiling for a moment while he summoned what were obviously remarkable powers of recall. 'The account was opened about eleven years ago at the Inverness branch, by Mr Cameron in person and in cash, with a deposit of eight thousand five hundred. A second deposit of four thousand eight hundred followed a year later. The remainder of the balance was made up of interest. Enquiries among the local shops revealed that the amounts had been raised from a major local jeweller, the first for a very good gold watch and the second for a pair of gold and diamond cufflinks. Neither seems to bear any relationship to the stolen goods on any list and the jeweller said that each item appeared to have been, if not brand new, certainly unused. He re-sold them through a colleague in Inverness.'

Stuart was looking as bemused as Grace felt. 'I simply do not understand it,' Stuart said at last. 'How would my uncle come by that sort of treasure?'

'That is hardly for me to speculate,' said the solicitor. 'I may have my hands full enough when it emerges that, apart from a legacy of five thousand pounds to his doctor, your uncle made you his beneficiary. Were you aware of that?'

'I had no idea,' Stuart said. 'And I didn't care. Sometimes he tried to put pressure on me by threatening to change his will, one way or the other. I told him several times that he would be welcome to leave his money any way that he wanted.'

'You told him so in front of witnesses?'

'No, of course not. That isn't the sort of discussion that you have over the teacups.'

'A pity. If the question should arise,' the solicitor said thoughtfully, 'and if you can stand up to questioning on the subject, I think you could include that in your statement to the Inspector. Beyond that point you don't go unless I am present.'

'Understood,' said Stuart.

When they had conducted Mr McCormick to his current-registration Mitsubishi Shogun and watched him drive away, Stuart said, 'Well, it beats me. How would the old devil have come by those sort of valuables?'

Grace helped him to re-enter the house. Steps still presented him with a slight problem. They returned to the sitting room. 'You'll notice that there were no items of lady's jewellery mentioned,' Grace said. 'But I suppose it's too small a sample to draw any conclusions from.'

'I don't get you,' said Stuart.

'I was just rambling. Your uncle spent much of his working life in the navy. He must have been in and out of foreign harbours. He must have got his hands on them abroad.'

Stuart pursed his lips. 'What you're saying – and you're probably right – suggests that they were stolen somewhere along the way. There's no way he could have afforded them otherwise. And that raises an ethical question. Can I and should I accept money from that kind of source?'

'Point one,' said Grace, 'the police will no doubt be following up on hallmarks and things and if you don't hear any more you can safely assume that they're clean. Point two, he could have come by them innocently. Let's say that, in some foreign country, or even in Britain, he found a lost suitcase and those were inside. He handed it in to the police but it was never claimed and in the end was handed back to him. That does happen, oftener than you'd think.'

'Why would he not have mentioned any such sequence of events to me? We were living in the same house.'

'It could have happened before he came to live with you. Or perhaps he thought that you saw the suitcase or whatever it was first and he was afraid that you'd claim any reward that was going.'

'But I don't remember seeing any suitcase.'

'Or a briefcase,' Grace said. 'Or a carrier bag. And you needn't even have seen it, he just might have thought that you had. I wish you wouldn't pick nits while I'm struggling to offer you explanations. Point three...'

'Yes?'

'I'll think about it. There is a point three but I haven't been able to think of it yet.'

Chapter Ten

Grace slept better than she had a right to expect and she awoke to a renewed belief in justice and the triumph of right over wrong. Giving Stuart his morning treatment, working on his well built body and feeling and sharing the improvement that every day brought, always worked a similar magic on her mood. A set of limbering exercises for her own body, a shower and a training session with Bonzo on the lawn confirmed her sense of wellbeing.

Halfway though the morning, she set off for the shops. Her step was light and cheerful, in tune with the gentle sunshine and a warm breeze off the sea. The season for tourism was almost past but the flowers in the window boxes and hanging baskets still glowed. This was the town where Grace had grown up but she had left it when she left her teens. She could never return to her teens but she had a sense of having come home. She was at one with the town. She was no longer a gawky and sometimes rebellious girl, she was a respectably married lady. She exchanged nods or smiles with those she met.

In the small supermarket, the shelves seemed to be arranged in no particular order. She was puzzling her way around the unfamiliar display of prices when a voice spoke in her ear. 'Grace Gillespie, isn't it? Grace Campbell now, of course.'

Grace looked round. The woman, of about her own age, was confronting her with a determinedly friendly smile. Her blunt features raised a distant echo in Grace's mind but the artificially fair hair made recall more difficult. 'I'm sorry...?' she said vaguely.

The smile remained fixed. 'Kathy Duvas. We were in the same class at the Academy. Don't you remember?'

Grace had a vague recollection of a girl with spots who in her one year at the academy had gathered a very differed coterie of friends. Grace was becoming practised at camouflaging lapses in memory. She stole a quick look at the other's left hand. 'Yes, of course. But I remembered you as being taller. And it's your married name that escapes me.'

The other looked mildly gratified. 'It's Reid. How do you like being back in Dornoch?'

'I love it.'

They chatted for a few seconds before Kathy broke away. 'Got to go. I'm meeting some of the old gang. You'll have to join us for coffee some time.' She slid between the few shoppers and left Grace mildly puzzled.

Grace resumed her shopping. She was interrupted by another face from the past but this time one that she recognised. She had always liked Molly Grange without ever becoming closer than distant friends. This, she seemed to recall, was because Molly preferred the friendship of boys to that of her own sex. She prepared for the air kisses, shrill laughter and meaningless chat normal to a meeting of old schoolfriends, but Molly surprised her. 'I've got to talk to you.' she said. 'I think it's urgent. Finish your shopping and come for a coffee.' She turned away and became interested in the loss leaders beside the checkout.

Anything still missing from Grace's basket could be left for another day. Grace paid for her purchases, transferred them to carrier bags and joined Molly on the pavement outside. They walked together to a small café a few yards away. It was pleasantly old fashioned, with dark wood where another café would have had bright plastic, and it was clean. Molly led her to a corner table and then doubled back to fetch two cappuchini.

They had the café to themselves apart from two women in the opposite corner. The younger, who had the hypnotised expression of a rabbit confronted by a stoat, was being lectured by her companion on the subject of the Evils of Men.

Molly nevertheless lowered her voice. 'I had to talk to you. I can't believe that you know the rumours that are going round and I wanted to warn you before you put your foot in it right up over your head. If you see what I mean.'

The impact of her words hit Grace like a blow. She had been blind, stupid, turning her back on the facts not to have seen it coming. She felt the blood draining from her cheeks but she fought the faintness. This was no time for weakness. 'I can guess,' she said, 'but tell me anyway.'

Molly took a sip of coffee. She was nerving herself for an

unpleasant task. 'Not everybody believes it,' she said. 'Those who remember you stand up for you, but that only keeps the argument going. The malicious gossips – and there are plenty of those around, you may remember – they're saying that you and your husband murdered his uncle.'

Now that it had been said aloud, it was worse. 'That's absolutely and totally untrue,' Grace said. 'How do they think we did it?'

Molly shrugged. 'That doesn't matter. You were a nurse, Stuart's a scientist. The police stopped the funeral and you're being investigated. People are being asked about poisons. That's quite enough to keep the tongues wagging. They can remember plenty of cases when the experts have disagreed about what killed somebody. People have done years in gaol and then been released with compensation, so it can't always be cut and dried, that's what they think.'

Grace leaned back and closed her eyes. A lorry rumbled past out in the street. Her mind was refusing to deal with this new crisis. She opened her eyes and looked at her well-meaning friend, taking in her appearance for the first time. Molly had a sense of style diametrically opposed to her own. Grace knew that she herself dressed well. She had been told so, often. But her choice of clothes tended towards the formal, the professional. She wore dresses or suits or skirts with tops. Nothing wrong with that but, now that she came to consider it, the result, while not unflattering to her figure, was always demure. Molly, she now realised, looked... sexy. There was no other word for it. How did she do it? He clothes did not look particularly revealing. But somehow they suggested that somewhere beneath them was rosy flesh and soft lace. Would Stuart prefer a wife like that?

Grace dragged her mind back. 'If the subject comes up again,' she said, 'you may care to mention that somebody had been robbing Mr Cameron's building society account while we were out of the country on our honeymoon. Lots of people could have got at his PIN number and lots of people could have given him poison or something. They have no call to pick on us in particular.' Her voice was in danger of breaking, She paused and swallowed.

'Why don't they pick on somebody else? Doctor Sullivan for instance?'

Molly seemed amused. 'I think you may find that he was away at the same time that you were.'

Grace had a feeling that Molly had been on the point of saying more but had decided at the last moment to hold her peace. She sighed. 'Anyway there isn't a lot I can do about it.'

'But there are some thing you can not do,' Molly said. 'I mean, things you can avoid doing. Why do you think Kathy Reid spoke to you just now?' Grace said nothing. 'She wasn't just after a friendly chat,' said Molly.

It came back to Grace that Kathy Duvas had been most notable as a source and transmitter of just the kind of malicious gossip that was now being bandied about concerning herself. 'She wanted to be able to repeat what a murder suspect said to her?'

'Come on, Grace. Do grow up.'

The dread penny finally dropped. 'Oh my God! She's hoping that I'll be arrested for murder and she'll be able to say, "I was talking with her only recently and she said to me..." Is that what you're telling me?' Molly was shaking her head. 'Worse? Dear God! You mean, if I'm convicted she'll boast about chatting with a murderess. That's disgusting! It's sick!'

'It's the way of the world,' said Molly. 'Or at least the sick part of it.'

'But what can I do about it?'

'I can't tell you what to do. I'm only warning you not to get drawn into conversations that can be twisted or misquoted or repeated out of context. If you try to brazen it out, you'll only keep stirring it up. In your shoes, I'd drop out of circulation for a while. Do your shopping somewhere else.'

'I think that's good advice,' Grace said thoughtfully. 'I'll probably take it. Thanks, Molly. You're a pal.' She managed a wry smile. 'And if I get arrested you'll be welcome to tell all our pals what the accused woman said to you.'

While they talked, Grace's mind had made occasional little darts towards escape and during those intervals she had become aware of the diatribe at the other table. The younger woman was a newcomer, which went a long way to explaining how she had come to fall into the clutches of the older woman, who Grace had by now recognised as Frances Nell.

Miss Nell was a singularly unattractive woman, being large and square with protruding teeth and very large feet. It was generally held that she was the stupidest woman in Scotland north of the Industrial Belt. There had even been a suggestion that she be put forward to *The Guinness Book of Records*, but the proposition had foundered over the fact that nobody dared ask her to sign the proposal form. She had been giving vent to a long lecture about the Wickedness of Men. Phrases such as *only after one little thing* and *after they've got what they want* dripped like acid from her tongue. It was all very sad, especially considering that no man had ever been after Miss Nell's little thing and probably none ever would.

Grace was suddenly aware that the other pair had fallen quiet and were gathering up their bags and chattels. The younger woman made for the door but Grace stiffened herself as Frances Nell headed in her direction, her face solemn but her small eyes glinting with anticipatory triumph at the cruel blow she was about to deliver.

She paused and leaned over Grace. 'How can you bear to live with yourself,' she demanded, 'after what you did to that poor old man?'

She had picked the wrong moment to tangle with Grace, who had taken quite enough from the world for one day. It was her turn to dish it out. 'How does it feel,' Grace demanded, 'to be the object of every man's desire?'

The blow struck home. No answer was possible. Frances Nell had never been the object of any man's desire but it would have been impossible for her to say so. It may then have come home to her that Grace's retort had about the same level of probability as her own slander, but more probably not. She stood still, open-mouthed but unable to speak while her face and posture slowly sagged. There were tears in her eyes and her nose began to run.

Grace became aware that Molly was making faces at her. She interpreted them as suggesting that Grace should get out of there before the quarrel exploded into a hissing, screaming, hair-pulling match that would delight the citizens of the town for years to come. As suggestions go, it seemed sensible.

Grace got out of the café, leaving Molly to pay for the coffees. She set off for home, lugging her shopping. Remembering her own words, her mood swung between satisfaction and regret. She, secure in the warmth and comfort of a glowing marriage, had no right to taunt the unloved. The warmth seemed to have gone out of the day and it seemed to her that every glance sent in her direction was an accusing glare. She kept her eyes to the front or she might have seen that, from the few people to be seen, some of the glances were sympathetic and that others were not directed at her at all. The scene was becoming misty.

Her way, which had seemed so short on the outward journey, now seemed endless and the hill precipitous. She arrived at last at the gate. Managing the latch and closing the gate again while juggling two fat carrier bags was almost too much. But the front door was open and Bonzo rushed to welcome her home. She put her bags down with care and snatched up the puppy, burying her face in the warm, dog-scented fur until she felt brave enough to face people again.

Chapter Eleven

A very much upset Grace gave Stuart an only slightly expurgated account of her morning. Stuart took the incident just as seriously, though his concern was as much with physical as with emotional consequences. He was on the phone to Mr McCormick immediately. Until the police completed their enquiries, Stuart said, rumours would continue to fly and it was not acceptable that his wife should be exposed to abuse. Moreover, in the normal course of events the next stage would be vandalism and the appearance of graffiti; and with Strathmore empty and presumably unguarded overnight it would be a vulnerable target. He wished it to be made clear that he would hold the police responsible for any such damage.

'You couldn't,' said the solicitor. 'Not unless you could prove malice or criminal negligence. You may be over-reacting. I certainly hope so.' A sigh could be heard over the line. 'But I agree that this has now gone on long enough. First, we should take a look and see what really is happening there. I am free this afternoon. Would you meet me there? Say two-thirty?'

'I still don't have my car back,' Stuart pointed out. 'Could you pick us up?'

'Now that really is too bad.' The solicitor sounded as annoyed as if his own car had been impounded. It seemed that kicking a young couple out of their home was acceptable but also to deprive them of the power of travel was, paradoxically, going too far. 'They've had plenty of time to collect dust and fibre samples and anything else that they deem relevant. In view of the nature of the crime as they perceive it, your car would seem to have little relevance. Leave it with me and I will see you this afternoon.'

That much settled, Stuart felt free to turn his attention to comforting Grace.

Shortly after two, the solicitor's Shogun drew up at the door. His practice, he explained as he drove up the long hill to the main road, often required him to visit outlying farms in wintry conditions and he had come to consider the ground clearance and four-wheel-drive essential. 'I have spoken to the Detective Inspector.

He admitted that these forensic science laddies hate to part with anything that might conceivably hold evidence. They would happily keep your car under lock and key forever; but the innocent private citizen still has some rights, even before being convicted of anything.' The solicitor emitted a humourless grunt. 'After conviction, of course, he suddenly has the full weight of the law to protect his rights and he can manage without my assistance. Your car will be returned to you not later than tomorrow morning.'

'And the house?'

'He wishes to meet you and to take a further statement from each of you. After that, he expects to return the keys. He proposes to meet us at Strathmore shortly. I accepted on your behalves. I trust that you approve?'

'Anything,' Stuart said, 'if he will only let us get on with our lives.'

'And if we're going to attract trouble,' Grace added, 'I'd prefer not to attract it in the direction of my parents. They've had their share of stress and they're entitled to a little peace.'

'In what you consider to be their old age,' Stuart added, 'though they'd be bitterly insulted to hear you say so.'

'I like to think that my own children will be as considerate,' Mr McCormick said, 'but I am not counting on it. I suggested recently to the older of my sons that if he is ever to adopt a family crest the motto should be *Money grows on Dad.*'

At Strathmore, two cars were already occupying tarmac. One was Stuart's own car, dusty but apparently undamaged. The other was a plain, unmarked Vauxhall which had, it seemed, brought Detective Inspector Fauldhouse. The door of the house stood open and the Inspector emerged into the sunshine and waited.

Stuart had now passed the point of needing help to get out of a car and the extra height of the solicitor's Shogun made the exit easier. He left his sticks in the car and walked to the door, stiffly but unsupported. Grace walked close to him, just in case. The Inspector had more *savoir faire* than to invite the Campbells into their own house. He stood aside. 'We've finished here,' he said. 'For all time, I hope. The technicians are only interested in results, not in clearing up after themselves, so Constable Brora is tidying your sitting room for our use.'

Grace was unsure whether such a service was part of the normal course of events or whether thanks were called for. 'We could sit outside,' she suggested. 'It's a lovely day and there's the swing seat and plenty of garden chairs.'

The Inspector seemed tempted by the unorthodox suggestion. He looked out at the gentle sunshine but in the end he shook his head. 'What we have to say would be better kept out of the public realm for the moment,' he said. 'Hedges have ears.'

The sitting room was now reasonably tidy and had been roughly dusted although traces of mysterious powders were still visible in corners. The open windows allowed a change of air but there was still stuffiness and a trace of a smell compounded of various chemicals and powders. A thorough spring clean was definitely due but Grace, seeing the room for the first time without the gloss of tidiness and lived-in quality suddenly saw it as dull and overdue for a total renovation. Even during the discussion that followed, part of her mind kept straying back to colours and fabrics.

Constable Brora, a stocky young man who Grace remembered seeing around Dornoch, seemed embarrassed at being found at housework. He rid himself hastily of a striped apron, originally the property of the late Mr Cameron but since appropriated by Grace, and produced the ubiquitous police notebook and a small tape recorder.

The Inspector went through the routine of recording the day, place, time and the persons present. 'I would like first,' he said, 'to ask Mrs Campbell what she can tell me about,' he refreshed his memory surreptitiously from a scrap of paper, 'succinylcholine chloride. Also known as Scoline,' he added helpfully.

The wandering part of Grace's mind came back hurriedly from the sweet pea range of colours.

Mr McCormick held up his hand and spoke quickly. 'Before Mrs Campbell answers, I think we should know the reason for the question.'

The Inspector hesitated.

'I should think that the reason is patently obvious,' Stuart said. 'The only possible reason for the question is that traces have been found in my uncle's body.'

'Almost right,' Grace said, 'but not quite. It's all right,' she added quickly to the solicitor. 'I've done nothing wrong and if I try to hide my very slight knowledge I'll only arouse unjustified suspicions. Correct, Inspector?'

'That's absolutely right.'

'Very well,' said the solicitor. It was already too late, he thought. He only hoped that his client was not about to produce some damning piece of expertise.

'Bear in mind,' Grace said, 'that I trained as a nurse and I worked for a short period as a junior theatre nurse. I have to dig back into my memory for lectures that I attended more than ten years ago but I'd be silly to deny all knowledge. Scoline is a muscle relaxant, which is very useful in some sorts of operation, because you sometimes get a muscle that stays taut or even goes on flexing while the patient's unconscious.' Grace paused and her brow creased with the effort of memory. 'It can have some bad side effects. It's used by anaesthetists because it acts very quickly – you don't want to suspend an operation while you wait for a twitching muscle to relax – but an overdose would leave the patient totally and permanently relaxed.' She paused while she raked through her memories. 'It's sold under a trade name – Anectine, I think or something very like it. I remember seeing the name on a label once. I think it's a white powder but I don't think I've ever seen it out of the bottle.'

'Why did you say that I was almost right?' Stuart asked.

Grace found that once she had begun to recall her lecture notes it all came trickling back. 'There was a case in New York some time ago and another in Texas. One of my lecturers referred to them in passing. He said that there were no direct tests for Scoline in a body but that it could be indicated by the presence of succinic acid in the brain. If I'm right and if science hasn't moved on since I was a student nurse, and also if my memory isn't leading me astray, I suggest that your logic, Stuart, points in that direction.'

Stuart nodded. 'I bow to my wife's superior knowledge and modify my earlier comment to suggest that succinic acid has been found in my... my uncle's brain.'

Grace looked at him sharply. There could be no doubt that Stuart was making an effort to speak dispassionately about matters that he must have found painful. She spoke quickly, to cover for him. 'There you are, Inspector. That's the limit of my knowledge and how I came by it. I have never used or handled the stuff, nor even seen it used as far as I'm aware.'

Inspector Fauldhouse seemed taken aback by such frankness. He was more used to witnesses who denied knowing anything about matters that were common knowledge than to one who volunteered knowledge of esoteric poisons. 'Apart from its use in anaesthetics and, occasionally, as a murder medium,' he said, 'have you ever heard of any other uses of Scoline?'

'Once again,' Mr McCormick put in, 'I think that you should tell us the reason for the question.'

'I would prefer to have the answer first.'

'I can assure the Inspector that I have never heard of any other use for Scoline.'

The solicitor smiled. 'Go ahead and ask the question.'

'Your client has already answered it,' said the Detective Inspector, 'so I may as well give you my reason. Many people hoard sleeping tablets or other relatively painless means of release, in case they or somebody close to them should ever face the prospect of a painful, terminal illness. I am speaking about suicide or euthanasia. Have you ever heard, Mrs Campbell, of Scoline being used for purposes of euthanasia?'

Grace's attention had begun to drift in the direction of carpets. The present carpet, in addition to being worn, was hideous. She would not want a carpet in Persian or Turkish patterns but something pastel and misty. She had friends in the hotel trade who could get her a bargain in quality. It took her a second to digest the question. 'No, never,' she said. 'Of course, doctors don't talk about euthanasia. It happens, of course. Quite a lot. No doctor worth his or her salt would let a favourite patient linger in agony. But the necessary doses of painkillers eventually add up to a level at which the patient will slip out of life. It's a fine borderline, often crossed. Doctors don't talk about it.'

'And nurses? Do they talk about it?' The Detective Inspector looked at Grace in a way that he probably considered penetrating.

'Do they talk about euthanasia? Sometimes, but without saying anything very interesting. Or do they commit it, you mean? A nurse would be taking a much more serious risk than a doctor. It may happen. It probably does. But I don't know of any cases.'

'You're quite sure of that?'

'Absolutely. And, going back to your earlier question, I wouldn't expect Scoline to be used in euthanasia of oneself or a loved one because it must be a less than pleasant way to die. You see, the muscle relaxant effect doesn't work on the heart but it does work on the breathing, so that unless that patient has a weak heart the death is by suffocation.'

Detective Inspector Fauldhouse scowled at her. 'But surely the effects of suffocation are unmistakable.'

'Not necessarily. And remember, Mr Cameron was an old man with not a lot going for him. The sudden arrival of a dose of what is in effect a poison may have been enough. You'll have to ask your medical advisers about this but my opinion, for what it's worth, is that he went too quickly for cyanosis or petechiae to develop. Sometimes, Inspector, a patient just plain dies. An elderly doctor who was half expecting him to suffer further strokes might easily be fooled.'

The Inspector was not going to be drawn into medical debate with a possible suspect. He changed course. 'Mrs Campbell, did you ever give Mr Cameron his medication?'

The solicitor opened his mouth but closed it again without speaking.

'I was often present and helped with the medication. He was a contrary old man and made things as awkward as he could.'

'The nurses say that you were sometimes alone when you gave him his medicines.'

'One moment,' said Mr McCormick quickly. 'Before Mrs Campbell comments – if she feels that your statement calls for a comment – I think you should tell us how you believe that any lethal dose was administered.'

'I can't tell you that,' said the Inspector.

'Then I advise Mrs Campbell not to answer the question. She doesn't even know whether you, or the nurses, are referring to medication given by mouth or by injection.'

The inspector's mouth was clamped into a thin line. He opened it to say, 'I can't tell you because I don't know. No traces of Scoline can be detected in the deceased's stomach. They have not found any needle punctures. But of course needle marks can be hidden in recesses of the body, in a pimple, under the hair line...'

'If it's of any help,' Grace said, 'the nurses were alone with the patient oftener than I was. So were the doctor and Miss Munro. For all I know, so was my mother. I'm only mentioning this because you're obviously playing the old game of telling witnesses that other witnesses have tried to incriminate them, hoping to get them all throwing accusations at each other. So you're welcome to pass on my comments, Inspector. For the record, I never gave him any medication except in the presence of at least one of the nurses and I never gave him an injection, nor saw one given to him.'

'You'll sign a statement to that effect?'

Grace was losing patience. 'Inspector, I'll put it to music and sing it.'

'That will not be necessary.' DI Fauldhouse turned to Stuart. 'Mr Campbell, were you ever present when medication was given?'

'Never,' Stuart said firmly. 'I found my uncle's condition very distressing. He had been a pillar of my young life, as good as a parent, and I hated to see him as an incoherent invalid. I didn't think that my presence was ever a comfort to him and when he misbehaved it was my wife who had the knack of bringing him under some sort of control. I wanted to remember him as he was in earlier years and I avoided seeing him whenever I could.'

The Inspector's eyes flicked to and fro between those of Stuart and Grace. 'To your knowledge, has there ever been Scoline in this house?'

'Definitely not,' said Stuart. Grace said, 'There must have been, if he died of it, but I never knew of any.' She went back, mentally, to choosing light fittings.

'That's all for the moment. You have your house and car back. I shall be asking you to come in and make formal statements when the case is a little more advanced.'

'We have the house and car back,' said Stuart. 'But what about my uncle's body? When can we give him the decent burial that you interrupted?'

'Not yet,' said the Inspector.

During Detective Inspector Fauldhouse's inquisition, Grace had been aware, at a low level of consciousness, of the arrival of a vehicle. The Inspector accorded it no more than a frown. When the sound of its arrival was not followed by a ring at the doorbell, it remained ignored.

The Inspector was running out of pertinent questions. That did not deter him from asking variations on the questions already asked and answered. That he received the same answers for a second or third time did not seem to surprise him in the least. He gave up at last. Grace escorted the two policemen to the door, mostly for the satisfaction of closing it behind them. The van from the landscaping firm had found space to park but was blocking in the police car. Grace left them to sort it out for themselves.

'You can see the problem Fauldhouse is facing,' Mr McCormick was saying as she returned to the room. 'Little or no scope for forensic science outside of pathology and none at all for house-to-house enquiries or fingertip searches or any of the other techniques beloved by investigators and enshrined in routine. He has indications of a poison that would, I presume, be obtainable only by those with some medical connection. No doubt hospitals and pharmaceutical wholesalers are being badgered to account for every grain of Scoline that has passed through their hands. Well, I wish them the best of luck with that one! He has one doctor and several nurses to consider; and each might be considered to have the possibility of a motive if one bears in mind the robbery from Mr Cameron's building society account. And he has that matter of the theft of money, which may or may nor be connected to the death, to account for, but if he can't trace the missing card I don't fancy his chances very much. I do not envy him his task. But he has a reputation for dogged determination, so we can hope for the best.'

Stuart roused himself from a reverie. 'One tends to forget the likelihood that somebody actually did this thing,' he said wonderingly. 'I have to keep telling myself that there may be a real person walking around who killed my uncle.'

'Unless,' said Mr McCormick, 'there is any way in which the poison – Scoline, was it? – could have arrived by accident. Or, of course, succinic acid in the dead man's brain. Mrs Campbell, you are the nearest that we have to an expert...'

'Don't look at me,' Grace said. 'I quite surprised myself by remembering as much as I did from my student days, but that really is the limit of my knowledge and I never was much of a hand at chemistry.'

'In that case,' said the solicitor, 'the only sensible course remaining open to us is masterly inactivity while we wait for DI Fauldhouse to do something clever. I will, of course, sit in on any formal questioning. Apart from that, I seem to have fulfilled my function for the moment.'

'One more question,' Grace said. 'The police have left the rest of the house in an awful state. Not just mess and untidiness. They've taken panels out and made holes in plaster. Don't they have to repair the damage?'

'Not if the search was being done lawfully and in good faith. If the original warrant was obtained by being economical with the truth, you might have a case. Shall I look into it for you?'

Grace could see the prospect looming of more fuss and bother and bad relations with the police. 'No, don't bother. I'll phone a builder. And our insurers. If our policy doesn't specifically exclude damage by the police we'll claim on that and let the insurers go after the police authority if they want to.'

'You're probably wise. Before I leave, perhaps I may take a look at the garden?'

'Of course,' Stuart said. 'I should warn you that it's not in a condition for inspection.'

'I understand that, but I'd like to see what Mrs Largs is making of it. I'm considering changes to my own garden at the moment and I may be able to steal some ideas.'

'You could always engage her yourself,' Grace pointed out. She had a particular liking for May Largs.

'If this case drags on for long enough, I may even be able to afford her,' said the solicitor. 'I'm joking,' he added.

'I sincerely hope so. I think the foreman from the landscaping firm is here, which may mean that the last two trees have come,' said Grace. She now had a clear picture of her mind of exactly how she wanted the sitting room to look and she desperately wanted time to make notes before the vision blurred, but she liked the solicitor. She let good manners overrule her personal wishes. 'Let's go and find out,' she said.

They left by the front door and walked round the gable of the house. Now that they were out of doors, Stuart lit one of his rare cigarettes. Mr Hodges was at work but he spared them hardly a glance. One tree, a while lilac according to the label, was already in place and tied to its stake. The tree was so flimsy compared to the stake that it made Grace think of Joan of Arc. On the other side of the garden, Mr Hodges was digging another hole. The small tree with its root-ball looked insignificant beside the barrow, several watering cans, sacks of compost and chemical fertiliser and another stake.

They did a quick tour of the garden. It required an effort of imagination to see it as it would become rather than as bare peat peppered with tiny plants, but Mr McCormick made appreciative noises. 'Give it a year and you won't know the place,' Mr McCormick said.

The tour was interrupted by the arrival of the two nurses. Grace met them at the corner of the house. 'The police have left us to it,' she told them, 'but the house isn't habitable yet. Give us a day or two and you can have a bedroom each.'

'But that's what we came to tell you,' said Janet. 'We're going away for a day or two. A lady who we nursed back to health and full mobility after a horse fell on her has invited us to come and stay for a couple of days and man the first aid tent at a gymkhana tomorrow.'

'We thought it would make a break from the police and questions,' Alicia said. 'The Inspector told us that it would be all right provided we left a phone number with him, didn't go anywhere else and came back in a few days.' She looked at Grace with large, dark eyes. 'It's been no fun for us but it must be terrible for you. We told the Inspector that you couldn't possibly have done anything to the medications.'

Grace was inclined to believe her. She awarded the Inspector a black mark for trying to mislead. 'He does seem to have his knife into us,' she said.

Alicia paled under her café-au-lait complexion. 'Mrs Campbell, that may be my fault. The Inspector was putting a lot of pressure on us and I don't know how it came up but I blurted out what you said on the phone, something about being going to kill that man. He was pressing me for every word that had been said and I knew that it was just the kind of thing you might say in irritation, not meaning it at all. It sounded awful after it came out but I couldn't call it back.'

'Did you include it in the statement that you signed?'

'He insisted.'

Grace wished the nurses a safe journey and saw them on their way before rejoining Stuart and Mr McCormick. She was in a pensive mood.

They were arriving back near to where Mr Hodges was at work. 'That's a big hole for a small tree,' Grace remarked.

Mr Hodges acknowledged their presence by nodding. 'They need root-room,' he said into the hole. 'I'll tease the roots out as much as I can when I plant it. And there's a clematis to go in beside this one. This is a viburnum, a snowball tree. The clematis will grow through it and they'll flower at the same time. It'll look very special,' Mr Hodges said reverently. He could become almost verbose when the subject was his plants. He took a spadeful of compost, added some fertiliser and spaded the mixture into the ground. 'Better give it some depth for a tap-root.' He exchanged the spade for a fork and drove it into the bottom of the hole. The tines struck something hard, producing a hollow sound. Mr Hodges turned over the earth. 'This'll have to do. I just hope I can put the stake in.'

'Hold on,' said Stuart. 'That sounded as though you might be on top of an old drain. I wouldn't want a tree put in where it's going to cause trouble later.'

Mr Hodges made a dismissive gesture. 'Not a chance. Your septic tank's over there,' he pointed, 'and the storm water drain runs beside the other, I know because we uncovered them while we were setting the new levels for the lawn. If there's anything here, it's older than your house.'

Stuart remained unconvinced. 'Even if it's a land-drain and older than Satan, we wouldn't want a tree right on top of it. Roots can find their way into a drain and block it completely. We'd hate to have our new garden flooded.'

'Mrs Largs said to put the tree in here,' Mr Hodges said, as if that were an end to the matter.

Grace had left Dornoch in the hope of being allowed into Strathmore; and in expectation of beginning a cleanup of a dusty house she had dressed accordingly. She decided that her cotton dress would wash as it had washed many times in the past, and her trainers would not take any great harm. 'I'll borrow your spade,' she said.

Mr Hodges seemed doubtful about leaving the digging to a lady. On the other hand, to dig on her behalf would have been a climb-down. He surrendered his spade and stepped away from the hole. Grace took his place and began to scrape and dig. Mr Hodges turned away and busied himself with unwrapping the root-ball of the tree and teasing out the minor roots. Mr McCormick wandered off and began reading the labels on plants. Stuart watched fondly as his wife dug and he wished that his knees would allow him to do the husbandly thing and take over for her.

Grace soon realised that she was digging around an object rather than along something linear like a drain, but it sounded too hollow to be a stone. She knelt down. The earth was dry and sandy and came away easily. She wished that she had gardening gloves – her nails would be in dire need of a manicure. But she plunged her hands bravely into the soil and found what felt like a pair of handles. She pulled. There was resistance, but she could sense that this was only the object's weight and that it was free of the soil. She stood up in the bottom of the hole, bent her knees and pulled.

What she lifted and placed carefully on the path a few seconds later was a container, apparently an urn. The loose earth brushed off easily. The solicitor squatted beside it. 'Bronze,' he said. 'I'm no expert, but I'd say English design, late eighteenth century. Plain but very elegant. No ornamentation except for a few acanthus leaves and a coat of arms, and it isn't one that I recognise.'

'There was a large stone right here,' said Hodges. 'I wondered at the time why it'd been left there when a man could have shifted it. It could have been marking the place for whoever buried it.'

'That seems likely. I remember the stone,' Stuart said. 'I thought that it was the top of a bigger rock.'

Mr Hodges had been thinking. His manner, which had been dull and slightly patronising, suddenly sharpened. 'Hey, is it valuable?'

'Tolerably.'

'Well, I found it. Just you remember that.'

'You can put that idea out of your mind,' Stuart said. 'You were going to plant a tree on top of it. My wife found it and dug it up. It was on our land. You've no claim at all. This is our solicitor. You can speak to him about it if you want to waste your breath.'

'Mr Campbell's quite correct,' said Mr McCormick.

Mr Hodges subsided, grumbling.

'Is there anything in it?' Mr McCormick asked. 'Or anybody?'

'Anybody?' Grace echoed. 'You mean…?'

'Look at it,' said the solicitor. 'What does it remind you of? To me, it recalls a funerary urn. It's rather on the large side for one person's cremation ashes, but that's what it looks like. Perhaps cremation wasn't as complete as it is nowadays when this was made. Did Mr Cameron usually double-trench for his vegetables?'

'Always, before potatoes,' Stuart said. 'He kept some beds aside for vegetables and rotated them around. He always double-trenched the bed where potatoes were to go. He couldn't have done that without striking the urn, so my guess is that he put it here for safe-keeping with the big stone on top to mark the place. In which case, it can't be somebody's ashes. It surely can't have been his way of getting rid of the body. It beats me what he could have felt he needed to keep secret from me. See if the top comes off, Grace.'

Grace took hold of the round cap. It resisted at first and then came away. She hesitated. Something awful could be lurking there. Was she releasing the genie? Or discovering the ashes of a murder victim? Everyone kept telling her what a charmer Mr Cameron had been, but it was common knowledge that charmers were the worst sort – think of Bluebeard. She looked and felt relief. 'It's full of papers,' she said. 'They're bone dry.'

'Money?' said Hodges.

'Letters,' Grace said. She took out the topmost bundle and unfolded it. The paper was heavy quality and the top page, which was headed by an embossed crest and an address, was covered by a small and elegant writing. It took only a glance at a random paragraph to discover the nature of the letters. 'Love letters,' she said. She replaced the papers and the lid. 'I think that we should take these indoors.'

Mr Hodges stepped forward as if to carry the urn but Stuart checked him. 'You're not concerned in this,' he said firmly. 'Finish planting the tree.' Hodges scowled but he picked up the fork and drove it into the earth with a force that would have skewered a second urn had there been one.

Mr McCormick picked up the urn. 'You must be stronger than you look,' he told Grace. 'This is heavy.'

'I work out,' Grace said simply. 'And in my profession, you learn to lift patients without straining yourself.' She and Stuart followed the solicitor round the house. Grace darted ahead through the front door. There was a discarded newspaper on the sitting room floor. Grace spread it on the coffee table and Mr McCormick thankfully deposited the weight of the urn in the centre.

'We'll wash our hands,' Grace said, and to Stuart, 'No peeking until we come back.'

'Trust me,' Stuart said. He picked up a cloth and resumed the interrupted cleaning.

There was neither soap nor a towel in the bathroom. They washed companionably, in cold water, at the kitchen sink. They found Stuart waiting patiently in the sitting room, happy to lay down his cloth and take a seat.

Grace felt only marginally involved. Old letters could only concern Stuart's family. There were more interesting things to consider in order to keep her mind away from Alicia's news. The suite would have to go. A visit to Dingwall or Inverness would be necessary. The new suite would have to be comfortable as well as attractive. Stuart could choose it and she would make sure that he sat in it for a lengthy period before a decision was reached. There would be no later complaints about lack of comfort. But she would retain the right of veto. She toyed with colours again.

'Before we begin,' Mr McCormick said, 'let me say this. It is a safe assumption that this was the property of the late Mr Cameron. You are his residual legatee and it may therefore be assumed to be yours now. Perhaps you should inform the executor, but I have no aegis in the matter and if you wish me to go and leave you to it I'll do so.

'However, first I should point out that this is no mere collection of old letters. The coat of arms on the urn matches the crest at the head of that first letter and the address – Oswald House – is well known. It is the house of a great lady, the Dowager Duchess Cecelia. The one letter that I saw was signed with the letter C. The question arises as to whether Mr Cameron could have been in legitimate possession of those letters. To your knowledge, did he ever have occasion to come into contact with minor royalty?'

'Part of his naval service was aboard the royal yacht,' Stuart said.

'And his given name was Duncan? That letter was simply addressed to D. I suggest that we should scan quickly through the contents of the urn and then consider what to do.'

Stuart said, 'I agree.' Grace, feeling only marginally involved, just nodded.

Chapter Twelve

Mr McCormick began to empty the urn. The neck was large enough to admit his hand with room to spare. At first, the papers came out in small groups, one letter folded around several as though, Grace thought, the recipient had waited until there were enough to justify the effort of digging up the cache. Later the letters emerging, presumably those written earlier, were in a loose jumble. They smelt musty, like the wrappings of a mummy.

While his hands were busy, the solicitor continued speaking. 'I recall some of the lady's history,' he said. 'I have the advantage of some years over either of you. At the time of her husband's death at sea, I was still young but not too young to hear some of the current gossip. It was whispered that the Duke was homosexual, which was not regarded as tolerantly in those days as it is now and would have been totally unacceptable in one of his rank. So, to still the gossip, he was hastily married off to Lady Cecelia. She was very young. There were some who doubted that she knew what she was getting into. Others said that wealth and noble status made up for any incompatibility in the bridal bed. When she bore him a son, the rumours died down; and at least he seems to have been discreet about his little adventures. All the same, I think that there was some general relief when he was lost at sea.'

He had laid the letters out in a roughly linear arrangement. They were written on a variety of papers and although the heavy cream paper of the first letter predominated Grace noticed that very few of them were on headed paper. That cream colour, she thought, would be very suitable for the room's woodwork. Not one letter was dated.

They began by reading what seemed to be the earliest letters, each reading one at a time in silence. 'This seems to be the first one,' the solicitor said suddenly. 'It's rather stilted and circumlocutory. She thanks him for his note and suggests that any future communications should be sent to her maid, Gladys Heffer. But she goes on to say that she too found their recent contact extremely pleasant and hopes very much that it will not be the last. She adds that she will be on *Britannia* again for the cruise to

Gibraltar the following month.' He looked up. 'I don't think that I'm letting my fevered imagination run away me if I suggest that, reading between the lines, this is the writing of a young woman starved of love both romantic and physical, who has experienced her first night of real passion, who wants more and is determined to get it.'

Grace was giving the letters her full attention. 'I don't think that your imagination's over-active,' she said, still poring over another letter. 'This one must be some months later and she seems to have gained confidence. She's becoming outspoken, even explicit. Pardon me if I blush.'

'I don't think that I'll even show you this one,' Stuart said. 'You'd turn purple.'

Some minutes passed in silence except for the rustle of paper. 'I feel like a peeping Tom,' Grace said. 'I'm intruding on something highly personal, romantic, erotic and rather beautiful.'

'You can read stronger stuff any week in *News of the World*, nowadays,' said the solicitor. 'In fact, this is comparatively – Oh my God!' he broke off.

'What?' said the others together.

'She refers to a difficult childbirth. She goes on – are you ready for this?'

'Tell us or don't tell us,' Stuart said. 'Either way...'

'Oh very well,' Mr McCormick said. '*Our child will grow up a duke and heir to my husband's fortune and estates.*' The solicitor blew out his cheeks in a silent whistle. 'There were always some questions as to the paternity of the present Duke although nobody dared to query it aloud in public. In my youth, there was a sort of gentlemanly agreement that the media would sit on any tidings that would be harmful to the nation. Those days have gone by and they will pounce on any such morsel today, provided only that it will sell papers. This seems to put the matter beyond doubt. It is to be presumed that she would know whether or not her husband could have been the father.'

'My cousin the duke,' Stuart said wonderingly.

Grace sat, half-stunned by the magnitude of the unfolding story. 'We have a decision to make,' she said at last. 'Do we burn these letters or return them to the dowager?'

The solicitor let out a long breath. 'I'm so glad that you said that. I was afraid that your attitude might be different.'

'I don't understand.'

'My poor innocent,' Stuart said, 'he was afraid that we might recognise the cash value of these letters. If one were to set up an auction involving the media and the establishment, the sky would be the limit.'

'I wouldn't even dream of such a thing,' Grace said indignantly, with only a fleeting thought of the cost of refurbishment. 'There have been quite enough scandals recently.'

'More than enough,' Stuart said. He sounded, for the moment, amused. 'You're a monarchist, then?'

'God, yes! Of course! Look at the countries that elect their heads of state and see what they get. Lechers, liars and warmongers. We might even get John Prescott! It doesn't bear thinking about.'

Stuart went back to reading. 'Ha!' he said suddenly. 'Here we come to the death of the old duke. I call him that to distinguish him from his... from the present duke. He was actually quite young. She dismisses him in about three lines and goes on, *The enclosed is a present that I bought for him but never gave because I was out of patience with his attitudes. I'd like you to have it, but sell it if you are so minded, I won't mind.* He seems to have waited a few years before turning it into cash.'

'I think that this one follows on, not very much later,' said Mr McCormick. 'Listen to this. *I believed that you were destroying my letters. Now you tell me that you cannot bring yourself to destroy these symbols of our love. My darling, that sentiment touches me to my heart. A part of me insists that our love is forever, the letters merely symbols. Yet another part can understand that you would hate to destroy any part of it. But you must realise that those letters must never, ever be seen by other, less loving eyes. They could destroy me and all that I've worked for. And they would ruin the memory of my poor husband, who never asked to be what he was.*

'*I have a suggestion that may answer. There is an urn that my husband brought back from one of his journeys. He intended it for his ashes but he was lost at sea (as you know well, having been one of the party that attempted rescue). I will give it to you next time we meet. This should be not long off, my dear, as I am due at Castle of Mey soon and can slip away. It is a strong urn and I believe it to be proof against damage. Keep my letters in it and bury it in your garden so deep that nobody else will ever find it. Then when we are dead and forgotten they can rot as we will have rotted. How suitable that the urn that was to have held the ashes of my husband will hold the ashes of the love that produced the son who bears his name!'*

'That's sad,' Grace said huskily. 'A great love, physical and romantic, just as we said, and all gone to ashes.'

'At least they had that love,' said Stuart. 'Few are so lucky.' Husband and wife exchanged glances.

Grace was smitten by sudden understanding. 'But this explains why your uncle got so upset when he realised that we were having the garden dug over and the levels altered.'

'So it does!' Stuart exclaimed. 'And it explains something else.' He got clumsily to his feet and fetched the leather picture-frame. 'Was this the lady?'

The solicitor studied the faded image. 'Yes, I'm sure it was.'

'On the back there's just one word written. Love. No signature. Not even an initial.'

'That would have been sensible of her, for once. Even if it fell into the wrong hands, it would be meaningless.'

They resumed their reading. Grace found that much of the material was repetitious, some of it mundane. By skipping quickly through the irrelevancies, she worked her way well ahead. 'It seems that their affair continued almost until the present day. In fact, there's a hint that when physical passion died they remained romantically attached.' She looked speculatively at her husband for a moment.

'That may have been when his temper began to decline. But, as you say, the relationship must have lasted. There was one wreath at the funeral that was unaccounted for,' Stuart said. 'Not ostentatious but very expensive. We assumed that there had been a card that became detached, but we never found a loose card.'

Grace was about to add some comment when she was distracted by a sound from the kitchen. She jumped up and darted through the hall. The back door stood open and Mr Hodges was filling a watering can at the sink.

'What?' Grace broke off. She had no wish to look as foolish as she certainly would if she asked him what he was doing. 'How does the back door come to be open?' she demanded.

He raised his eyebrows at her. 'I was here earlier and those bobbies opened it for me. I had to water in what I planted yesterday, didn't I? Then I got a call that your last two trees had come so I went to fetch them and brought them back. Now I'm giving the new plantings a good drop of water. I shan't need any more today, so you can bolt the door.' He lifted his can out of the sink and stalked out into the garden, the picture of injured dignity. Grace closed and locked the door.

Stuart and Mr McCormick were at the hall door. 'Was he listening?' Stuart asked.

'I don't know. He's down the garden now. Did he seem indignant enough when I questioned his presence? He has quite a temper and I expected him to blow his top.'

'There's nothing to be done about it now,' Mr McCormick said. 'Except, perhaps, to be more careful.' He led Stuart back into the sitting room but Grace remained where she could watch Mr Hodges through the kitchen window. 'Let's consider the next steps. These letters, after all, would be meat and drink to the media and would raise all kinds of complications regarding the dukedom. Really, she must have been mad or obsessed to put anything on paper at all. She's a very beautiful lady with a great deal of wealth, charm and influence. She works hard for some very good causes but nobody ever said that she was first in the queue when intelligence was being handed out. Luckily, the present duke isn't in the direct line of succession or I think we would have to take some action, though I can't for the life of me think what.'

'I think that you should take custody of the letters,' Grace said through the open door. 'You would know better than we would how to return them to her.'

'I agree,' Stuart said. 'The letters are hers but the urn is ours. It was given to my uncle and found on our property and I'm not parting with it. Grace, can we find a box to put the letters in?'

'I'll accept the custody of the letters and the duty of returning them to the lady,' the solicitor said. 'I agree that we would have no right to destroy them. The only outstanding question is, do we tell the police?'

'Good Lord, no!' Stuart said. 'I think that we three could keep the secret, but if we told the police the papers would have the story next day. It's nothing to do with them.'

'I think you're missing a very important point,' said Mr McCormick. 'The recipient of the letters may have been murdered, shortly after suffering a serious stroke.'

'I don't see any connection between the two events,' Stuart said slowly.

'I don't think you want to see any connection,' Grace said. 'But it's there. I can see two possible connections straightaway without even guessing which of them Mr McCormick is referring to. Firstly, it could be argued, Stuart, that because these very valuable documents would come to you, you might have had a motive for inheriting them.'

'Ouch! And the other?' Stuart asked.

'The other would be that after his stroke, which was a bad one, somebody might have been afraid that your uncle's mind might have been wandering and he might have let out the truth or led somebody to the letters. From the viewpoint of the establishment, his death might have been an improvement.'

There were sounds from outside. Grace walked through the room and looked out of the window. 'That's Mr Hodges away,' she said. She resumed her seat. 'I'm certain that the first theory doesn't represent the truth. As to the second, suppose that that is what happened. I don't think it is, but suppose it anyway. Never mind the motives. Who has been harmed? Your uncle wasn't robbed of a life worth living. I can see that to tell the police would be to stir up a real hornet's nest. On the other hand, if we return the letters straight away they're lost to us forever. If, later, the police decided to prosecute somebody that we knew was innocent – perhaps even one of us, Stuart – we could no longer use the letters to provide an alternative explanation. I suggest that Mr McCormick keeps them in his safe or at the bank, or anywhere just so long as it's a safe place. They can be returned to the dowager once Mr Cameron's death is explained.'

'You can leave that aspect in my hands,' said the solicitor. 'A very confidential approach, offering a return of the letters against a promise of support might meet the case. Let me think about it.'

The telephone sounded an old fashioned ring, making them all jump. Grace rose and answered it. She listened. 'Yes, Mother,' she said. 'We'll be setting off for home in a few minutes.' She hung up and looked at her watch. 'Gosh, is that the time? No wonder my mother's getting anxious. Give me a minute to phone the builder and put repairs in hand. While I do that, Stuart, there's a box of about the right size for the letters among my electric stimulators.'

As Grace put Stuart through the passive part of his treatment the following morning, she managed to isolate one aspect of the situation that had been worrying her. She said, 'I suppose Mr McCormick is to be trusted? I mean. There's a lot of money could be got out of those letters and solicitors are only people. They have been known to fall from grace.'

'Rather often,' Stuart agreed. 'They're exposed to more temptation than most of us. They're trusted to hold large sums of money for ancient or deceased clients and then as often as not they prepare the final accounts – and in a form that even qualified accountants have difficulty in understanding. But I don't think that we have to worry too much about Andrew McCormick. My family switched to him for legal work because of a case he was involved in. It turned out that he had been offered a huge bribe to present evidence that he, and only he, knew to be untrue. He turned it down flat. Client confidentiality prevented him speaking out at the time but somebody talked and the facts came out at the subsequent trial. We can take it that he's honest.'

Grace rolled him over and flexed his knees, one at a time. His mobility was still improving. Returning to Dornoch the previous evening, Stuart had managed to drive his own car safely and even with a touch of his old style. 'I just can't picture your uncle as a charmer,' Grace said. 'I don't think that I ever met anyone with less charm. Of course, I never met him until a few months ago.'

Stuart had to turn his head to speak past the pillow. 'By the time you arrived, he was a crotchety old man who was probably depressed by coming to the end of a long and joyous physical affair and then having to face up to all the aches and pains of old age. He was my mother's older brother, and she married late, so he was a lot older than I. But I still remember him as kindly and wise, always neat as the proverbial pin and, looking back, I suppose he was good looking with it. He was funny, too. I remember, when I was very young, he pretended to have his finger stuck up his nose. I thought that it was hysterically funny at the time, but most things are either tragic or funny to a seven-year-old and those are the kind of things that stick in your mind. I suppose that his libido and his sense of humour died at the same time. The one followed the other.

'He was very courtly to the ladies and they seemed to melt at the sight of him.'

'So that's where you get it from,' Grace said.

'I wish you meant it. If only I'd had the knack!'

'You wouldn't have settled for me?'

'Ouch! I'm delighted that I settled for you. It's the best choice I ever made. I'm only being wistful about the bachelor life I could have enjoyed if I'd been able to melt girls with a single glance. Anyway, his charms were a few years back.'

'More than a few.'

'All right, more than a few. But how many is a few? I don't think he was promiscuous. He may have made special efforts to keep me in the dark, but I don't think so. From all the signs, he had his chances but he was faithful to his one-and-only. I always knew exactly where he was except that he used to go away for days or even a week or two at a time. He was supposed to be sea fishing with an old friend, but now I suspect that any fish that he brought back came off the fishmonger's slab. Those would have been the occasions when his ladylove managed to steal some time to be with him.'

'That seems likely.'

Grace fell into a reverie about the long-running romance. She tried to imagine an affair conducted in extreme secrecy. Her imaginings may have been coloured slightly by the fact that in nursing attendance on the old man she had noticed that he had once been remarkably well endowed by nature.

Her parents had already been advised that they were about to lose their guests again, but it had been decided that they would allow one extra day so that Grace, aided by her mother, could get Strathmore fit for occupation while Stuart visited his school to check that all was ready for the coming term.

In mid-morning, Grace sent Stuart on his way with a stern warning to drive safely and that if he began to experience the least difficulty he was to phone Grace on her mobile and then wait for her to come and drive him back to Dornoch. When he had managed to travel out of sight without any noticeable faults, Grace felt free to load her mother's car with the necessary supplies and cleaning materials and the two set off.

Such was the nature of the dowager's secret that Stuart and Grace hasd decided to say nothing about the letters. The urn itself, however, could not be hidden forever. It would be a feature of their home – indeed, Grace was already imagining it in the refurbished sitting room, filled with flowers from the remodelled garden. The urn had been carried back to Dornoch and duly admired. The explanation that it had been empty when discovered in the garden was accepted without question. Grace felt slightly guilty about lying to her parents, but the cause was a good one.

'Maybe the vase was buried with some valuables hidden in it,' Mrs Gillespie said as she drove slowly over the long bridge. 'And somebody helped themselves to the contents later.'

'Perhaps,' Grace said. It was not very far from the truth.

'It'll be Roman, likely.' History had never been Mrs Gillespie's strongest subject.

When they came within sight of Strathmore, Grace sat up suddenly. A blue and white police car was stopped in the road beside the gate. Mrs Gillespie braked to a halt a good stone's throw short, to the great inconvenience of a van driver who had been following hard behind her.

'Whatever can be up now?' Mrs Gillespie said.

'If you don't drive on, we won't know,' Grace said. 'You've got room to turn into the drive.'

Her mother pulled forward. As the car entered the drive and the van went past, Grace saw that the front door was standing open. A small pane of glass beside the door had been broken. DS Ballintore emerged from the house, approached quickly and stooped to the car window 'Mrs Campbell, we've been trying to reach you but your mobile isn't switched on,' he said reproachfully. 'There was a break-in during the past hour.'

'I must look,' Grace said. She opened the door, forcing the Detective Sergeant to step back, and hurried into the house. One or two cupboard doors stood open. Otherwise, the house was much as they had left it. A quick tour satisfied her that Stuart's two computers were still in place as were her few items of jewellery and those pieces of physiotherapy equipment that had not been removed to Dornoch. Anything else could be replaced at modest cost. In fact, she intended to enjoy replacing the carpets and curtains, but those remained stubbornly in place. A little assistance from the insurance company would not have gone amiss. Really, these days you couldn't even count on a burglar to do a thorough job.

DS Ballintore had followed closely behind during her tour. 'Well?' he said. 'Well?'

'Just a minute.' Grace went round again more slowly. 'There's a bottle of whisky missing,' she said. 'I'm fairly sure that that's all.'

Mrs Gillespie had joined them. 'My Lord!' she said. 'They've fairly messed the place.'

Grace hid a smile. 'This is pretty much how the police left it,' she said. 'The builder's coming.'

The Detective Sergeant flinched. Her mother avoided comment except for a pursing of the lips. 'We'd better get started,' she said.

'I'm sorry, Mrs Gillespie,' said the DS, 'but Mr Fauldhouse is on his way and he wants to see it as it is.'

'Just sit down a minute, Mother,' Grace said, 'I'm going to make a phone-call from the car. The Sergeant,' she explained carefully, 'won't want me putting fingerprints on the phone. Who's the nearest glazier to here?' The DS made no objection as she hurried outside and extracted her mobile phone from her bag. Mr McCormick's secretary answered on the second ring but it took Grace half a minute to persuade the woman to put her through.

The solicitor came on the line at last. 'There's been a break-in at Strathmore,' Grace said. 'We weren't there, we planned to move back in tomorrow. The urn was with us in Dornoch.'

'And you're guessing that they were after the letters? That seems to be a strong possibility.'

'But do I tell the police?'

'No,' said the solicitor after a pause. 'I think you don't.'

'But...'

'But there is a possibility that the break-in is connected to the letters and a very remote chance that the letters are connected to Mr Cameron's death. It really is a rather tenuous connection. There is no certainty that the information would help them to clear up the mystery of Mr Cameron's death and an absolute certainly that any revelation would bring scandal down on the head of a great lady who either chairs or is patroness of a number of worthy causes. I think... Yes, I think that you had better leave this to me. Avoid the whole subject and if necessary consult me before making any admissions.'

'I can do that. Can you put me back to your secretary?'

Mr McCormick's secretary looked up the glazier's number in the yellow pages for her. She was speaking to the firm when another car rolled up and DI Fauldhouse emerged. Grace followed him inside as soon as she could. 'The glazier will be here this afternoon,' she said. And if they cared to assume that that head been her only call, so be it. 'Good morning, Inspector,' she added. She took a seat beside her mother but the officers preferred to stand.

The DI acknowledged her greeting with a nod but spoke to the Sergeant. 'Tell me,' he said.

DS Ballintore referred to his book. 'Call received at ten-thirty-five,' he said. 'Car attended. I was notified and, because this house features in a current case, I followed up immediately. Neighbour, Mr Munro, presently unemployed, heard glass break. He was otherwise engaged...' the Sergeant glanced at the two ladies and Grace guessed that Geordie had been on the toilet, '... but hurried round a minute or two later. He found a broken pane and the front door open. As he entered, somebody left by the back. He was not quick enough to get more than a glimpse of a man's back in dark clothes, but he heard a motorcycle depart in the direction of Bonar Bridge. He called nine-nine-nine immediately. The car followed up but there was no sign of a motorcyclist except for a lady on a moped who could account for herself. I was unable to contact Mrs Campbell but she arrived shortly after-wards. She states that nothing is missing except for an unopened bottle of whisky.'

DI Fauldhouse listened impassively to this recital and then turned to Grace. 'Well, what was he after?'

Grace trod down an immediate pang of guilt. The DI could not possibly have heard about the letters. 'I haven't the faintest idea,' she said. 'I don't have much jewellery and what I have is still here, what I didn't have in Dornoch with me. The most sellable things still here, I suppose, would be Stuart's computers, his CDs, the television and the hi-fi, but you'd know that better than I would. I haven't counted the CDs but otherwise they're all still here and anyway they'd be too big to carry off on a motorbike. Maybe he was going to make off with Stuart's laptop in a haversack or a pannier, but Geordie interrupted him.'

DI Fauldhouse looked at Grace with reproach. 'Mrs Campbell, we are in the middle of a murder case and somebody breaks into the probable locus. Is that coincidence?'

Grace forced herself to take time to think. 'I think it probably is,' she said. 'Coincidences happen all the time. You tell me that somebody poisoned my husband's uncle and I have to accept your word on that.' The Sergeant's moving pencil was distracting her. She paused and waited for the thoughts to clarify. 'If some-body was already robbing Mr Cameron's building society account, the culprit can't possibly have wanted him dead because you can only withdraw so much at a time from a cashpoint and the account was far from empty; and also because the death would be bound to expose the theft. If Mr Cameron had lived for another few years, it might never have been noticed at all. Nobody knew that the money was there and it would have become very unlikely that anyone at the building society would ever notice that Mr Campbell had been in hospital at the time of the withdrawals, And I can't see any possible connection with this break-in.'

'I suggest that somebody wanted to remove or cover up some evidence.'

'If Stuart or I wanted to do any such thing, we wouldn't have to break in,' Grace pointed out. 'Anyway, you've already removed or searched for all possible evidence.'

'We thought that we had. Our investigation has taken a step forward during the last day or so.' The Inspector paused and stared at Grace again.

Grace was becoming rather tired of the Inspector's cat-and-mouse tactics. 'Well? Are you going to tell us? If not, please go away.'

Detective Inspector Fauldhouse showed no reaction. 'Very well,' he said grimly. 'But I think that Mrs Gillespie might be spared the details.'

Grace's mother humphed. 'I was a theatre sister before I married,' she said. 'I'll be bound I've seen more gruesome details than you have, Inspector.'

'Very well,' said the Inspector again. 'The pathologist had proved to his own satisfaction that no Scoline had been given either by mouth or by injection, despite the presence of succinic acid in the brain. He says that he was on the point of admitting defeat. Then one of his students suggested that the suppository might have been the vehicle. The pathologist admits that he called the boy an idiot but then had second thoughts. It was quite possible. As soon as the gelatine melted, the Scoline would be absorbed quickly into the bloodstream. Paralysis, especially of the breathing, would be followed rapidly by cardiac arrest. The long and the short of it is that they carried out several tests and found a trace of Scoline solution in the prostate gland. I'm told that a suppository would be easy to tamper with. But somewhere there should be traces of that tampering.'

'I wouldn't be too sure of that,' said Mrs Gillespie. The others looked at her in surprise. Her motherly appearance had not suggested an aptitude for medical detection but as a nurse and a mother she had acquired a down to earth attitude to bodily functions. 'The suppository has gone where all suppositories go,' she said bluntly. 'It's been a long while since I was in an operating theatre, but I recall that Scoline was highly soluble in water. It would be as easy as winking to draw out the contents of a suppository with a hypodermic syringe and replace them with

Scoline the same way. And then what traces will you be left with? The gelatine would have melted in the body's heat and any marks on its surface would have disappeared. The syringe is disposable and went out in somebody's rubbish last week. Or it could have ended up in the Firth or simply been left in a public toilet somewhere. The staff would only dispose of it, thinking that somebody had been – what is the expression? – shooting something.'

'Up,' Grace said. She smiled fondly for a moment at her mother's naïvety but the smile was wiped away in an instant.

The Inspector accepted Mrs Gillespie's advice without comment and looked at Grace. 'Was Mr Cameron given any medication by injection?'

'Inspector, you know that he wasn't.'

'Did you see anybody with a hypodermic syringe in or near the house?'

'No, never.'

The memory of that fatal day was returning to Grace with awful clarity. 'Inspector, accepting for the moment that you're not aiming to mislead us, it seems that I may have given Mr Cameron the fatal dose. I can only say that I was absolutely, totally unaware that I was doing so.'

DI Fauldhouse made no direct comment. 'We shall be asking similar questions of everybody who was in the house during the last week of Mr Cameron's life, roughly the period during which the suppositories were there. Suppose that one of them says that you had a syringe or were seen otherwise tampering with a suppository?'

'They would be lying,' Grace said firmly. 'Or possibly mistaken. Bear in mind that I came back from my honeymoon only two days before his death. That hardly gave me time to obtain a syringe and a supply of Scoline – although I suppose you'll argue that it can't have been a spur-of-the-moment crime.'

The Inspector refused to be diverted onto this line of argument. 'You personally returned all Mr Cameron's medication to the doctor's surgery?'

'All except the aspirins, which were in the bathroom cabinet here until the SOCOs removed them. That's pretty much what

I've done in the past when a patient has died. I believe it to be normal practice.'

'Did you see anything to suggest that any of the remaining suppositories had been tampered with?'

'Nothing at all. I didn't even open the box.'

'Have you ever had Scoline in your possession?'

'Never.'

'What was your attitude to Mr Cameron?'

'I can see what you're getting at, Inspector,' Grace said hotly. 'Mr Cameron, by the time when I came to know him, was a crotchety and demanding old man. Even before his stroke, he was hostile. He never wanted Stuart and myself to develop a relationship. After his stroke and when the hospital more or less dumped him on us, it was obvious that he was going to be a burden, but it was a burden that I was prepared to take up for my husband's sake. I did not wish or do Mr Cameron any harm. I regret his death because my husband is saddened, but there's no denying that our life may be more comfortable for his going.'

Inspector Fauldhouse looked steadily at Grace. She managed neither to fidget nor to still the normal small bodily movements or to show any other sign that might be taken for guilt. She tried very hard not to think about the letters. The Inspector transferred his gaze to Grace's mother. 'Mrs Gillespie,' he said, 'did you ever see a hypodermic syringe in this house?'

'Never.'

'Or Scoline?'

Mrs Gillespie snorted indignantly. 'Not that or any other lethal poison.'

The Inspector looked again at Grace. 'Where is your husband this morning?' he asked suddenly.

'He went to his school, to see that all's ready for term-time.'

'Have you told him about the break-in?'

Grace shook her head. 'No. I've only just heard the details. I was planning to call him now.'

'Please do so. Tell him about the break-in and ask him to stay where he is for the next hour. Please limit yourself to the break-in and don't say anything about the other matters.'

Grace did exactly as she was asked, from the landline phone. As soon as the Inspector and the Sergeant had left, she called Stuart again from her mobile. Then she and her mother got to work on the house. They developed a rhythm of sweeping and dusting and washing-down. The arrival of the builder to repair the damaged panels and plaster, and then of the glazier to replace the broken pane, they took in their stride. The house began to look like a home again but Grace was still holding in her mind the mental picture of the changes that a fresh décor might bring. In particular, it might banish the memory of Duncan Cameron and especially the manner of his going.

Chapter Fourteen

Mrs Gillespie was a noted cook and her fish dishes were especially admired. The two nurses, however, had pretty well emptied the freezer at Strathmore, finishing the several trout that Stuart had caught at the mouth of a burn that ran into the Firth and stored in the freezer prior to his fall. It was therefore to a tasty shop-bought sole that they sat down that evening.

'That policeman thinks that you had something to do with Mr Cameron's death.' Mrs Gillespie said. 'Of course, he doesn't know you as we do.'

Grace, under the benign influence of a good meal cooked by somebody else, although still reluctant to consider the details of Duncan Cameron's death, was in a tolerant mood and prepared to consider its implications. 'Thank you,' she said. 'Of course, you can see it from his point of view, He doesn't have much to work on at the moment. Lots of people could have tampered with the suppositories. I suppose that the nurses had the most opportunity but I run them a close second – or third, whichever way you count it – and the nurses had no reason to want him dead. Nor had I, really, except that I want whatever you want. The Inspector's left with motives...'

'Which is never a good basis for a case,' said Mr Gillespie. 'It's often pointed out that when a mugging occurs almost everybody had motive but only one person, or two at the most, is guilty.'

'Perfectly true,' Grace said thoughtfully. 'But, if pressed, I'd have to admit that I had more motive than almost anybody. People keep telling me what a charmer Mr Cameron used to be but I never knew him in those days. By the time I met him, he was a cantankerous old autocrat. Neither of us made any secret of the fact that we disliked each other. After his stroke he got worse – I think the part of his mind that got damaged was the bit where self-restraint lives, along with inhibitions. I didn't wish him dead, but now that he's gone I feel a hypocrite whenever I'm obliged to say that I'm sorry. Unfortunately, I said something rash about being ready to kill him, on the phone to one of the nurses, and the Inspector heard about it.'

'Oh dear!' said her mother.

'That's putting it mildly. Then he had his stroke and, although I was quite prepared to devote my time to looking after him, I saw it as a duty rather than as a pleasure. There's no denying that I'd rather continue living my own life, including both being Stuart's wife and doing physiotherapy for private patients.'

'And, to save you saying it,' said Stuart, 'harsh though it sounds, we're better off financially and in other ways for his going. I had some lingering affection for the old man but I'm not blind to the changes that had come over him or to the effect that he was going to have on our lives. The fact remains that neither of us had anything to do with his passing.'

The subject was allowed to drop but in the privacy of their room that night Grace said, 'I'm worried.'

'Tell me why. Say it aloud. That often helps to clarify your thoughts.'

'All right.' Grace paused. She had almost finished disrobing. 'Two grounds. First, miscarriages of justice have been known to occur; and an apology and a sum of money can't make up for several years taken out of your life.'

'It won't come to that,' Stuart said.

'Can you promise me that? Stuart, people have been convicted on less evidence than they already have. Read the papers. Time and again I've though that they surely couldn't convict on such circumstantial evidence. Then the jury think that it couldn't be anyone else and anyway the police wouldn't have brought the case if the person wasn't guilty. Secondly, the police are working without all the information. Those letters would change the whole picture of motivation. Quite apart from the cash value in blackmail or to the media, it's only too easy to come up with a conspiracy theory. It may or may not be coincidence that several people who were rocking the Establishment boat have met with serious accidents in recent years, but there's no doubting that from the moment your uncle had his stroke he could have seemed to be a loose cannon.' She paused and gave him a friendly slap. 'You needn't smile in that superior way. I can mix my metaphors if I want to and, anyway, a boat small enough to be rocked could still be large enough to carry a small cannon. You knew perfectly well what I meant,' she said severely. 'I love you dearly but sometimes you can be a little too much the depute headmaster. If he had dropped dead, the dowager might have shed a tear but there would have been little other reaction. A stroke patient, on the other hand, can be irrational. In fact, he remained rational enough to be very worried when he realised that the garden was being remodelled, but they wouldn't know that.'

Stuart was being distracted. 'Come here.' Grace approached and Stuart pulled her down beside him on the bed. 'The sexiest thing about you is that you are a bundle of amazing contrasts,' he said throatily. 'You're graceful and dignified. Stately, I called you once. So when you throw aside your dignity or stand around looking like something out of the calendar on a garage office wall, you drive me out of my mind. Apart from the obvious action – this one – we'll do nothing for the moment. Anything else we do could turn out to be wrong. And when you can do nothing, there's no point worrying about it. So help me out of these trousers and we'll turn our attention to things that really matter.'

Grace, as always, was happy to oblige.

In the morning, Stuart's estate car was loaded. Farewells were exchanged and promises of invitations to dinners. Stuart had resumed his male prerogative of doing the driving. He stopped in the middle of Dornoch and accepted Bonzo onto his lap. Grace bought fresh supplies while facing down some curious stares. She knew that she was innocent and she wanted the rest of the world to see that she knew it.

'I have a great fondness for Dornoch,' Grace said as they reached the main road, 'but I'm glad to be getting out of it for the moment. I was beginning to feel like a goldfish in a bowl. With all this talk about your uncle's death I suppose eyes were bound to follow me around. Perhaps it's only my imagination that sees suspicion in them and hears tongues wagging.'

'It's much the same at the school,' Stuart said. 'The bolder boys even ask me direct questions about it. It's in their nature to be inquisitive and forthright, but they do go over the top at times.'

'I'm sure they do. But at least they wouldn't dare to throw things at you.'

She felt the car wobble slightly as Stuart reacted to the shock. 'Nobody threw anything at you, did they?'

Grace gave a little snort of laughter. 'No, of course not. But I always had the feeling that they were just about to.'

It was a dank and misty morning. Dew still lay wherever the road was shaded. Stuart drove with care.

Strathmore was quiet. They had never thanked Geordie Munro for his foray against the intruder so they shut Bonzo in the kitchen and walked along together. Geordie was not at home, but Grace was glad of the chance to assure Hilda that she had never for one moment suggested to the police that Hilda might be implicated in Mr Cameron's death. They left messages of thanks for Geordie with his sister and turned back. Violet Sands came out of the house between but when she saw them near her gate she turned back indoors with a mime of having forgotten something.

'It's going to be like that until somebody's caught,' Stuart said.

'I'm afraid so. We'll just have to grin and bear it.' Bonzo, who had seldom if ever been left alone since being separated from her siblings, greeted them with a rapture that helped to dispel their despondency.

They opened windows to let the dust and the past blow away together, but soon closed them against the damp. In addition to what they had removed to Dornoch, the car was carrying most of Grace's treasures. She forbade Stuart to carry any of the heavier cases, insisting that his joints were not yet ready for heavy weights but, while she grunted under the weight of the boxes, Stuart made several trips with lighter loads. After his first trip, Grace saw that he had lifted the bronze urn and placed it oddly off-centre on the sitting room mantelpiece.

'Do you plan to balance that with a clock?' she asked curiously. 'You'll see.'

When she next had occasion to visit the room she noticed that he seemed to be standing expectantly by. She looked at him closely but there was nothing about his appearance except for a half-hidden smile. She took one look around the room and let out a yelp of outrage.

Flanking the urn now stood a beautifully framed enlargement of his photograph of Grace with the green statue. It had turned out superbly. The colours were bright and true, the detail needle-sharp, the tones crisp and bright. Only rarely, even for the best photographers, do the details of an outdoor composition turn out to be artistically perfect. Grace's pose and her wicked grin had brought the statue to life. The scene carried conviction, inviting the viewer to share the delight. The green man was now clearly on tiptoe, almost levitating, dancing in a state of ecstasy, climaxing to Grace's caress. It was wild and provocative. It was beautiful. Even Grace's modest swimsuit was transformed, somehow suggesting exiguous underwear. The scene had become the distilled essence of humorous sexuality.

While she stood, now struck dumb, Stuart preened himself. 'Good, isn't it?' he said complacently. 'I must show it to your friend Jenny. She isn't the only competent photographer around here.'

'If you ever show that to anybody,' Grace retorted, her voice shaking, 'anyone whatever, I will never speak to you again.'

'I was thinking of using it for our Christmas card.'

Grace knew that her leg was being pulled but she was unable to stop. She heard her own voice, in a much higher tone than its usual contralto, ranting on. 'You can put that thought a long, long way out of your mind. I suppose I can't stop you keeping it in the privacy of your study or our bedroom and gloating over it when you're alone, but nobody beside the two of us is ever to see it. Do you understand?'

'I thought perhaps your mother —'

'Especially my... Oh, God Almighty, who's this?' She looked out of the window but whoever had rung the bell was out of her sight. A large and shiny car had stopped on the road.

'I'll go,' Stuart said.

'Don't bring them in here,' Grace said urgently.

She intended to remove that photograph from any possibility

of public view, but first she stole a glimpse from the doorway. Past Stuart's shoulder, she saw a well-dressed gentleman, hat in hand, and heard him, speaking. 'I am one of the royal equerries,' said that individual. 'We understand that some papers turned up, pertaining to a lady of noble birth —'

While sending Stuart a telepathic message to keep this individual talking, Grace slipped round the corner of the hall and into her bedroom where she could speak unheard. Her bag was on the dressing table, her mobile phone came immediately to hand and she had already installed Mr McCormick's number so that she had only to key two digits to hear his office number ringing. The urgency in her voice must have communicated itself, because the secretary put her through at once.

'Mr McCormick, there's a gentleman here saying that he's a royal equerry or something and wanting to know about papers.'

'Tell him nothing and give him nothing. I'm making tentative enquiries over a discreet route and nothing could possibly be resulting yet. I suspect that our gardening friend may have recruited an accomplice.'

'Thank you,' Grace said. 'That's all I wanted to know.' She dropped the mobile into her bag. As she paused for thought, she heard Bonzo yap sharply somewhere in the house. The puppy had been exploring her new territory. With the acute sense that dogs often show, she had already divined that this was home and must be defended against intruders. She had given the postman a nip on the ankle. The yap turned into a yelp.

Grace dropped her bag on the bed. Quickly but cautiously she emerged into the hall. Stuart, with his back to her, was still engaged with the stranger at the front door. They seemed to have reached an impasse of some sort. The sitting room door, which Grace was sure she had left wide, was almost closed. She pushed it open. Bonzo, who had retired behind the couch, gathered courage at her mistress's appearance and began barking again.

A burly figure in dark, rough clothing and some sort of a hood was standing at the mantelpiece. His hands were on the urn but he seemed to have frozen in shock. Grace flinched as she realised that what had stunned the man, driving all else out of his mind, had been the impact of setting eyes on the photograph.

Later, Stuart pointed out that the wise course might have been to allow the man a few seconds in which to discover that the urn was now empty. Grace told him that he had twenty-twenty hindsight.

'What are you doing there?' she cried. Not the brightest question, she admitted later to Stuart, because what he was up to was perfectly obvious. But that hardly mattered because at the same moment she was overtaken by fury at the sight of an intruder with the urn, by which Stuart set such store, in his thieving hands. She rushed forward.

The intruder jumped to meet her. He was holding the urn by one handle. He swung it towards Grace's head but, either out of reluctance to kill or from a gentlemanly disinclination to brain a lady, he checked the swing and turned his rush into a football-type barge, shoulder to shoulder. Grace was flung back, fell over the coffee table and landed on her back.

She forced herself to get to her feet but some seconds had gone by. She thought that she was unhurt except for being partially winded. She dragged air into her lungs and limped to the door. Her face was wet but she remembered receiving several sympathetic licks from Bonzo's tongue. The discussion at the front door had halted but she soon saw that the two figures had turned and were looking through the hall. There was a sound from the back of the house and she remembered that when Geordie Munro had disturbed an intruder the latter had run round the house. Her breath had returned. She plunged through the front door, brushing Stuart and the visitor aside.

There was no immediate sign of the intruder, but between the garden and the adjacent field was a hedge backed by a fence. She recalled a gap in the hedge and fence and a path, probably made by deer, leading up the side of the field to the road. They had been telling each other that the gap must be closed before the worst of the winter brought the deer down from the hills looking for easy pickings. The door of a vehicle slammed, suggesting that this time at least there was not a motorbike to be pursued. There was no time to run after it but Grace's mind was made up. She was determined not to lose contact with Stuart's precious urn.

Stuart's estate car was in front of the house, the key still in the dash in readiness for locking the car when the unloading was finished, and the gates were open. Grace leaped inside. The warm engine started at the first touch. Grace found reverse and shot backwards into the road with a confidence and a trust in her guardian angel that she could never have mustered in the ordinary way. No traffic was coming but she nearly ditched on the far side of the road. Nearly but not quite. A pickup van was departing in the general direction of Bonar Bridge and she set off in pursuit, one wheel spinning on the greasy tarmac.

A thin rain had started, the first proper wetting of the road for days. On the accumulated rubber and diesel slick, the surface was treacherous. The car should have had the legs of the van but Grace could make a guess at what Stuart's reaction would be if she bent his car. Wondering on which Stuart put the higher value, his car or the urn, she decided that the car might or might not be the more valuable but it would certainly be the easier to replace. She drove well within her competence and the car's adhesion. The pickup also was being driven with caution. The result was a slow-speed chase that allowed Grace time, at last, to think.

Her first thought was that the simultaneous arrival of a caller and an intruder was unlikely to be coincidence. Almost certainly the respectable gentleman was, as Mr McCormick had suggested, an accomplice, intended as a distraction if the direct approach should fail. Then it struck her that the back of the pickup was familiar. And then, belatedly, the penny dropped. Despite the balaclava, she had recognised the burly figure. Mr Hodges, the foreman from the horticultural firm, the man who had been beside her when she dug up the urn, who had undoubtedly seen the topmost letter and, she was now sure, had been listening from the kitchen while Mr McCormick told the tale of the dowager. Mr Hodges who was renovating a house although, as she had been told, he was a gambling man and always in need of money.

That realisation in turn raised a strong suspicion that Mr Hodges had been the culprit who had robbed Mr Cameron's building society account. Hodges could have stolen the card and seen Mr Cameron's note of his PIN. He had undoubtedly been inside the house from early in the garden contract – he had admitted having seen kitchen equipment that was not visible from the window. It began to fit together but she could still not see him as the murderer. The method was wrong and the motive was missing.

The police must not be involved, that much remained true. She hoped that Stuart had not reported the intruder to the police. But she was still not going to let the urn out of her sight. She gritted her teeth and held the car straight as the van ahead did a spectacular tail-wag.

The driver of the van – Hodges – must have been aware that he was being followed. Grace was kicking herself for having left her mobile phone behind, because at least it would have enabled her to speak to Stuart. Hodges would not know that she had been so foolish. He must be aware that she would have recognised the van. He would probably expect the police to be invoked. If he were thinking logically, which was far from certain, he would be aiming to get clear of the pursuing car before the police could halt the chase. He could then hide the urn, along with what he would believe to be the contents, and have a bargaining counter. In which event, they might never see the urn again. It would be his word against hers, and he was not the one under suspicion of murder.

Grace had no intention of overhauling her target. Stuart's estate car, she knew, was a much-loved artefact, prized beyond its cash value. It still glowed with the loving polish that it had been receiving up until the day of Stuart's accident. There was no question of playing dodgems with it. The chase might come down to a matter of who had the fuller tank. Grace looked. The needle was below half. She began to piece together a map of the area in her mind. There were not many filling stations. Was there one on a road with no junctions, where she could fill up without losing touch with her quarry? She thought not.

They were coming to the head of the Firth. At Bonar Bridge, Hodges could turn back towards Dornoch or go left towards the wilds in the direction of Ullapool or even Cape Wrath. Either vehicle running out of fuel in that desolation would be there for a long time. But, to Grace's relief, Hodges turned off into a maze of small roads around Ardgay. He hesitated at a junction which, Grace knew, would have brought him to a dead end at Amat Forest, but changed his mind and took a minor road that paralleled the other beside the River Carron.

Grace stuck doggedly to his tail.

Hodges managed to control another slither over a humpbacked bridge and then turned off onto another minor road. This one would allow him to get off the unclassified roads and back onto the network of A-roads in ten miles or so.

The road had been laid out by whoever designed the corkscrew although Grace, whose previous acquaintance with it had been from the saddle of a push-bike in her brother's company when she was aged about ten, found that the hills were now not the almost insurmountable switchback that she remembered but the bends were as sharp. The Kyle of Sutherland was below them if she had had the leisure to look down on it, but mostly they were climbing through a dark tunnel of trees.

Beech and silver birch began to be replaced by Scots pine and spruce plantations and grass gave way to heather and bracken. The road was now a single-track with passing places. Grace began to long for another vehicle to approach and block the way. With luck it might be driven by somebody helpful – somebody, at least, who could be persuaded to relay a message to Stuart. What Stuart would do to resolve the situation was unclear but she could rely on him to think of something clever. Perhaps he knew a local farmer who could be telephoned to block the road. But it was not to be. When at last a battered and rusty four-by-four appeared over a crest it coincided with Hodges's arrival at one of the passing places. Grace had to spurt to get through on Hodges's tail and the battered vehicle shot away again with a rattle and a backfire before she could catch the driver's attention.

The chase was brought to an end, just beyond a crest, by a fat woman on a bicycle who came wobbling out of a gateway. The van's brake lights flared, but on the down-slope Hodges had no chance of avoiding both the woman and the verge. The van slithered and the right rear wheel went down into the ditch. The driver's door was deep in prickly gorse. The fat woman shook her fist, shouted something and then sailed away on the downhill stretch.

Grace drew up beside the van, halting the car with some difficulty. Rain, it seemed, was now falling on cow-dung spread thin by traffic, but she controlled a skid while calling down a blessing on the designer of ABS. Victory was being handed to her on a silver salver. The van's nearside window was down and the urn was on the passenger seat, one handle conveniently within reach. Grace grabbed. The urn was heavy and the angle awkward, but haste lent her strength. Hodges made his own grab, but he was too late. Grace had the urn. She let the car jerk forward and was careful to put the inevitable dent from the urn into the van rather than the car. The urn was sturdy enough to look after itself. She changed hands and lowered it into the passenger's foot-well.

The car was still only crawling. She looked in the mirror. Hodges had erupted from the van as soon as she was clear of its passenger door. She saw that he had removed the balaclava as having outlived its purpose. He was tearing after her, his exposed face a mask of fury and frustration. Aided by the down-slope he was gaining on her fast. She tapped the accelerator. She could have shot away and left him stranded. But she had rather gone off Mr Hodges. She was sure that he had kicked Bonzo. She tramped on the brake. The car tried to stand on its nose. Hodges, unable to stop on the greasy surface, thumped into the flat back hard enough to shunt the car forward. Grace let the car roll a few more yards and then braked again. She got out, more to inspect the damage than for any other reason. But the damage to the car seemed negligible.

Hodges was lying on his back, his knees drawn up, gasping like a stranded fish. His nose was badly out of place and his lower face was a mask of blood. Grace, who was no longer friendly disposed to Mr Hodges, approached with no more intention than to do a little more damage. A physiotherapist knows where to land a good boot. But that might be to put herself in the wrong. She considered taking hold of his damaged nose and helping him to his feet with a good pull. But Hodges was totally winded. His eyes popped and his tongue was protruding. If he did not get air soon, brain damage would follow. Grace rolled him onto his side and then, using all her remaining strength, raised him into a kneeling position. Grasping his ankles, with a mighty pull she straightened him out. His breath returned with a whoop and he began breathing again. His colour returned from purple through puce towards scarlet.

As he was rolled over, a wallet had come out of his hip pocked. Grace did not care to search a furious man who might recover the power of motion at any moment. But the wallet might contain evidence and could be posted back to him. She took it with her into the car, dropped the wallet on the passenger seat and pulled away. As she overtook the fat woman, she gave her a friendly wave.

Rather than attempt to re-pass the place where Mr Hodges, if he were sufficiently recovered, would be trying to seek help or by his own efforts to extract his pickup from the ditch, Grace drove on, crossed the River Oykel by way of the low bridge and rejoined the road back through Bonar Bridge.

Almost an hour had passed since her precipitate departure from Strathmore. Arriving home, she saw no sign of Hodges. All seemed peaceful. Stuart had brought out a folding chair and was waiting for her, looking only mildly anxious, which Grace felt was less than flattering. It came to her that Hodges was probably in a worse state of fear than herself. Her knees, as she quitted the car, felt like rubber. She realised then that she had just driven more than thirty miles through just the kind of glorious scenery that she had yearned for during her long absences and she had never taken her eyes off the tarmac to spare it a glance.

Stuart rose and hurried to meet her. He seemed to be alone except for Bonzo. Grace, emerging from the car, stooped to pick up and reassure the anxious puppy. Bonzo seemed to be undamaged. Grace put her down and held up the urn. Stuart's face cleared. 'What happened to your visitor?' Grace asked.

'He buzzed off in a hurry. What happened to you?'

'I thought he might.' Grace was beginning to feel drunk with success. 'The two of them were in cahoots, whatever a cahoot may happen to be. One of them keeping us busy at the front and one sneaking in through the back. I'll tell you all about it.' Grace carried the urn inside, hoisted it with an effort and replaced it on the mantelpiece. She saw that during her absence he had accomplished most of the tidying-up. The photograph still occupied its place of honour, glowing with disreputable colours in the otherwise muted room. She ignored it. In her moment of triumphal return, she was above such petty indignities. 'That was Mr Hodges that I chased away. He put a dent in your car.'

'With his van?'

'With his nose.' She helped Stuart to lower himself onto the couch and they sat close, side by side.

'Tell me.'

When Grace had told the tale in detail they went outside again. A smear of blood led Stuart to the damage. 'I'll pay for a repair if you like,' Grace said anxiously. 'Save your No Claim Bonus.'

'No need for that, bless you!' He gave her a quick kiss and led the way back inside. Grace brought along the wallet. 'The door frame took most of the impact,' he said. 'There'll hardly be a mark once the blood's polished off. I'll treasure the bruise as a minor but honourable wound. What comes next?'

'I think it's what they call a Mexican standoff. He can't make a fuss about his wallet without owning up to trying to steal the urn and involving an accomplice. We still don't want the police so we can't call them in, though I suppose,' Grace said thoughtfully, 'that that's what he'll expect us to do, or even to have done by now. He got away with a lot of money from your uncle's building society account. But we'd have a job proving anything and he'll certainly have lost it gambling by now. You didn't see his face today, so it would only be my word against his.'

'We'll have to think about it. I have some of those thin polythene gloves in the car, the ones that garages give you to keep your hands clean? Would you mind?'

Grace fetched the gloves from the door pocket and Stuart opened the wallet. 'Nothing of great interest,' he said. 'Not enough money to be worth impounding against what he got away with. One credit card. A library ticket. Postage stamps. Forecourt receipts. One or two business cards. A Customer Reward Card from a DIY shop – which is just the sort of thing that a man might jot down a number on if he wanted a scrap of paper in a hurry.' He looked up. 'I suppose you wouldn't remember my uncle's PIN number?'

'As it happens,' Grace said, 'I would. The Inspector quoted it and I remembered. It was oh-two-two-four. Easy to remember of itself and it happens that it was the Aberdeen dialling code before they mucked about with it.'

Stuart produced a grin of triumph. 'Then we do have some proof. He jotted it down here. His fingerprints will be all over it. The trouble is, he could argue that he was jotting down the Aberdeen code, except that this reward card is dated after the STD code changed. I think we need Mr McCormick.'

'Leave it to me to summon him.' Grace snapped her fingers and made what she felt to be a suitably necromantic gesture. Through the window she had seen the solicitor's car arrive and she was still feeling a little light-headed after her successful venture against the horticulturist. 'That's fetched him. A little light witchcraft,' she explained. She hurried to the door and brought the solicitor into the sitting room.

'You bring him up to speed,' Stuart said. 'I'll make some coffee.'

'It's lunch-time. Bring some paté and things through here. You can carry them?'

'No problem.'

When she turned back into the room, Grace saw that Mr McCormick was standing frozen in front of the photograph. Damn! She had again forgotten to move it. To move it now would only impress it on his memory. Instead, she sat down and cleared her throat.

Mr McCormick seemed to shake himself. He gave a small snort and then found a seat. 'My office has gone quiet for once,' he said, 'and what there is is deadly dull. Your phone-call sounded much more interesting.'

'Perhaps it is.' Grace told the whole tale again, filling in details in answer to his questions. By the time she had finished, Stuart was putting down a large tray with toast, paté and all the makings. He went back for a second tray of coffee and crockery. 'I see that you're going to be the ideal husband,' she said. She looked at Mr McCormick. 'You'll join us?'

'Delighted to.' The solicitor began anointing strips of toast with butter, Brussels paté, mustard and finely chopped salad while he spoke. 'It happens that I know a certain amount about your Mr Hodges and it's true that he's perpetually in need of money. The conclusion would seem inescapable that he had access to your house during the early stages of the landscaping contract. He must have prowled around, looking for anything negotiable, and found the card and the PIN number. Knowing that Mr Cameron was unlikely ever to manage his own affairs again, he tried to solve his cash problem by robbing the building society account, but Mr Cameron outwitted him by dying before he'd got his hands on more than a fraction of the balance. Later, he witnessed your discovery of the urn and glimpsed at least one of the letters. Obviously there was big money to be gained so he decided to lay hands on the urn, not knowing that the letters had already been removed from it.' He broke off and took a large bite.

'That's exactly how we see it,' Stuart said. 'It accounts for everything except my uncle's death. Hodges would have been the person who most wanted my uncle to stay alive. But where do we go from here? In my view, the cash isn't too important. It would have been very useful but we can manage without it and we still have a useful sum to come; it just sticks in my gullet that he gets away with it. What do you think?'

'I agree,' Grace said.

Mr McCormick swallowed and patted his mouth with a paper napkin. 'Leave that aspect with me,' he said. 'I act for his older brother, who owns the firm. A respectable man. We may be able to work something out. Would you settle for free maintenance of the garden in perpetuity?'

Stuart glanced at Grace. She shrugged. 'I suppose so,' Stuart said. 'I love to sit in a garden or to watch somebody else working in it, but I hate gardening as an activity for myself. I'd want the work done by somebody other than Hodges junior.'

'Very well. If we discount the thefts we are, as you say, left with the death of your uncle. Assume for the moment that the police interpretation of the autopsy results is correct – although we can probably argue to the contrary if it should suit our book later. Murder by suppository *per rectum*. That strongly implies some-body who has a morbid imagination and has, or once had, a med-ical connection – you can't walk into the local pharmacy and buy ricin or scoline off the shelf. Of course, as the Inspector sug-gested, many people do keep lethal substances available in case of the need for euthanasia or escape, so anybody who has ever had a hospital connection may be suspect. That would include yourself, Mrs Campbell, the two nurses, the doctor, even possibly your mother.'

'And of all those,' said Stuart, 'apart perhaps from my good lady here, the doctor is the only one who had a motive, a finan-cial one. But one would suppose that an elderly doctor who has headed a practice for most of his adult life in a rural area, would have provided adequately for his retirement, which must be imminent.'

Mr McCormick, who had filled his mouth again, merely shook his head.

'I'm afraid not,' Grace said. 'Mother tells me that he was divorced a few years ago. Unwisely, he fought the action all the way and lost. The costs must have cleaned him out. Even a com-paratively small legacy might look very attractive.'

The solicitor looked at her with a sudden frown. He finished his toast slowly and emptied his mouth before speaking. 'This line of discussion opens up what for some strange reason they call a whole new can of worms. Now that you put the thought into my head, it occurs to me that the doctor has lost several well-off patients in recent years. And rumour has it that he has received a bequest or two. Whether there's any connection I wouldn't know. People do leave bequests to the last person to give them comfort, which is quite likely to be their doctor; and, to a doctor, the murder of a patient is probably the easiest mur-der in the whole field of homicide. Among other factors he, or

again she, is in a position to certify the death as natural. A dispro-
portionate number of serial killers have turned out to be medical
men... and women, especially nurses. Don't you ever quote me,
because I'm being professionally indiscreet, but I think that the
good doctor would bear looking at.'

It was Stuart's turn to look unhappy. 'You're right about the
can of worms. That sums it up nicely. Can we really throw that
kind of accusation at a respectable doctor.'

'You don't know that he's respectable. Doctors are always
thought of as respectable. The profession as a whole is
respectable, but the individuals? Think about medical students
for a minute.' (Grace thought. The most dissipated acquaintances
in her past had been medical students.) 'Think of the number of
doctors struck off for lewd and libidinous behaviour. After my
own profession, I believe that doctors are in the category most
exposed to temptation. But the police have so little to go on at
the moment that this case may easily end up open but unsolved.
In that eventuality, your good lady will be guilty in the public
imagination forever. Would you want that?'

Stuart made a dismissive gesture. 'No, of course I wouldn't.
Even so, and even if Dr Sullivan is a serial murderer, I don't see
how we could hope to make a case if the police can't make any
progress.'

Mr McCormick had picked up an apple but he deferred taking
his first bite. 'My dear young man,' he said, 'you are still missing
the point. You would not have to prove anything. The police
began investigating your uncle's death because of the thefts from
his building society account, which we have just decided were
coincidental. But that investigation was sufficient to start the
rumours. Now imagine if the police should start investigating a
series of deaths, including this one, because the doctor, whether
guilty or innocent of murder, had received a legacy from each of
the deceased and the death certificate in each case had been
signed by him or one of his partners.'

'The heat would come off,' said Stuart. 'Always provided that
people knew about it.'

'As you say. And we could make sure that they knew about it.'

The solicitor bit into his apple.

Grace had been aware of anxiety, like the first darkening of the sky before a storm, but suddenly it was as if blue sky was showing. 'You've suggested a wonderful way out for us,' she said, 'even if it is a bit hard on the doctor. How do we go about it?'

'First of all,' said the solicitor, 'we need to know which of his patients have died and which if any of those have left him a bequest. You can leave that bit to me. I can get copies of wills from the Books of Council and Session at Meadowbank House, provided that the testator is already deceased. Copies of death certificates can be had from the local Registrar. If we find even one name, other than Mr Cameron's, figuring in both lists, we have a starting point. In the meantime, you could, if you wish, start to gather up any other possibly relevant information about the doctor and his practice.' Mr McCormick looked at his watch. 'I must rush,' he said. 'I have a client conference shortly, but I'll get somebody started on some phone-calls. Excuse me. Thank you for the lunch.' He cast one more disbelieving look at the photograph and hurried out to his car, carrying his apple.

'Damn it!' Stuart said. 'I wanted to ask him what was happening about the letters.'

Grace hurried to turn the photograph to face the wall. The letters were of secondary importance.

Chapter Fifteen

Given at last a chance of positive action instead of passive endurance, Grace's immediate impulse was to rush to the doctor's surgery, on some pretext such as having her ears syringed, and start snooping. More mature thought assured her that precipitate activity would be certain to do more harm than good. She deferred action until the morrow.

Stuart was already engaged by telephone in a heated discussion with the school secretary over stationery supplies for the coming term. This, Grace knew, could and probably would go on forever. She took herself out into the garden. The rain had stopped. Nature had not made any dramatic leaps, but nor did anything seem to have died. The plants stood, each on its disc of dark, moist peat, as they had since they were put in. Even the plants that had wilted at first now stood up straight and pretended to be tall. Grace managed to convince herself that one small Japonica had put on an extra leaf. She walked round with her eyes half closed, envisaging. There were gaps in her knowledge of flower colours and the labels were not always clear as to which sub-species had been selected, but in the end she managed to build up what she thought was a realistic picture of how the garden would look in mid-summer. This activity was the perfect foil to the other half of her mind, which was sifting and re-arranging the mystery of Duncan Cameron's death.

May Largs had made the most of the limited space, which was generous by suburban standards but tiny compared to the gardens of gracious homes. The lawn was already showing a haze of green and its informal shape had been cleverly adjusted so that it would look, when the shrubs were up, far larger than its real size. The flowering trees around the perimeter graded down into shrubs and then ground cover underplanted with bulbs and tubers to give the maximum of harmonious colour for the minimum of maintenance. The curved terrace would provide a choice of sun or shade at most times of the day. The bottom of the garden was open to the view of the Firth and the mountains beyond, but a clever change of levels would suggest that the garden continued beyond its real boundary. Grace had approved the designs on paper without quite believing May's sketches. Paradoxically, she found the blitzed earth with its immature scraps of planting more convincing.

Spring, she decided, would be fun. The winter jasmine would not flower this year, but there were snowdrops to come and daffodils. After that, it would all begin to happen.

The garden part of her deliberations was interrupted by the sound of a car. Rounding the house, she found Janet Willoby's car in the driveway and the two nurses extracting themselves stiffly. She greeted them cheerfully. 'So, how was your break?' she asked.

'Restful, mostly,' Alicia said. Her teeth flashed for a moment in her dark face. 'Those riders who fell off mostly seemed to land on something soft, so the worst we had to deal with was a nosebleed and a trodden-on foot.'

'The media seem to have lost interest in Mr Cameron,' Janet said. 'So we were able to put aside negative thoughts and concentrate on rest and recreation. We still have a few days before we're due to go to Bristol and the Inspector made us promise to come back to answer any more questions and sign our statements. We're booked with the Munros for a few days.'

'Come in for a minute anyway,' Grace said. 'There's something I want to ask you.'

Stuart was still on the phone in his study. They could hear his voice rising as he laid down the law to the unfortunate school secretary, who was responsible for both the budget and the provision of supplies – a combination of responsibilities that made the lady sometimes feel, as she had told Grace, like the rope in a tug-of-war. Grace took the nurses into the sitting room. Bonzo climbed onto her knee. That was a habit that would have to be broken long before she attained her full size, but for the moment Grace let her off with it. A warm puppy is a great comfort when times are troubling. 'You know about the Scoline and the... the means of giving it?'

Alicia's eyes shone white again as they widened. 'That Sergeant came to see us, along with a local cop. If they're right, somebody has a nasty turn of mind. We said the suppositories hadn't looked as if anybody had messed about with them. We just got them in a package and opened it and used them. I didn't notice anything different from the usual.'

'Nor did I. And we don't know anything about Scoline,' Janet said. 'I've heard of it, that's all. I never knew of there being any within miles of here.'

'There's a few other elderly patients died while we were nursing them,' said Alicia indignantly. Grace thought that she was probably flushed with anger under the dark skin. 'Of course there were. It's bound to happen. Sometimes we're taken on to keep the patient comfortable during their last few days or weeks. But that Sergeant said they'd be looking into those cases, maybe doing an exhumation. He was looking at us as though we were going to break down and confess to something.'

'So we told him to get lost,' Janet took over. 'We said that we'd come back here and make formal statements, in the presence of a solicitor, and they could investigate anybody we'd ever nursed and welcome. We've done nothing wrong. We're meeting the Inspector tomorrow.'

'If you don't have a solicitor, Mr McCormick's acting for us,' Grace said helpfully. 'He seems very good. Of course, he may feel that there's a possible conflict of interest.' She paused a moment, waiting for her train of thought to clarify. 'The Sergeant didn't get as far as asking you how the suppositories arrived?'

Janet shook her head. 'We'd already told him to beat it before he got round to that. I don't think it would help much. When we found that Mr Cameron was having difficulty passing stools, I phoned the doctor and he said that he'd send some along.'

'He phoned back later,' Alicia said. 'I took the call. The surgery was out of them and he was phoning the wholesaler to send a month's supply direct to us.'

Grace felt a chill up her back. If the suppositories had been sent from the wholesaler, it seemed certain than any tampering must have been done at Strathmore. It was hardly likely that the postman had the skill or the motivation. 'Give me the details,' she said. 'I suppose the wrapping will have gone to the dump ages ago,'

'Maybe not,' Alicia said, frowning. 'I unwrapped the package when it came. Mr Cameron didn't have to pay for his prescriptions anyway and I'd said that one of us would sign the slip next time we were in touch with the doctor.'

'The wrapping paper.' Grace said. She tried to keep her voice calm.

'Oh, yes. There were postage stamps on it, and not just the usual ones. Well, you don't get many stamps these days, what with the e-mail and franking and all that, and I have a niece in Tobago who collects. I was going to cut out the stamps to send, but first we had a gift to take with us for Mrs Tinnings, for remembering us and putting us up – a china ornament from that tiny antique shop, you know the one. So I used the paper to wrap it. And when we got to Lanark, I took out the ornament and left the paper in the bottom of the case. I think it's still there. Would you like me to drop it in to you?'

Grace felt hope begin to stir again. 'Would you do that? It might be a waste of time but it could be very important. Do you remember anything else about the delivery?'

Alicia shrugged. Janet said, 'No. There wasn't anything.' Nevertheless, she put her mind to remembering. 'The suppositories were in a cardboard box with just the maker's name printed on it. You took it back to the surgery yourself. It held thirty suppositories in five rows of six. Or six rows of five, whichever way round you looked at it. And it was in brown paper, not a jiffy bag or bubble wrap.'

'And the last one that we gave him was – what? – the fifth or sixth out of the box?'

'About that,' Alicia said. 'If you get his charts back from the doctor, we could tell you exactly.'

Grace sighed in relief. It seemed likely that only one suppository had been doctored, on the safe assumption that the patient's treatment would get to it some day. To doctor more than one would be to ensure that a deadly and damning piece of evidence stayed behind. For a moment she had had a heart-stopping mental picture of another patient suffering constipation and the doctor opening his bag. 'Here we are,' he was saying. 'This will put an end to the problem.'

'Did Mr Cameron get anything by hypo?' she asked aloud.

'You know he didn't,' Janet said.

'But before I came home?'

Janet lifter her haughty nose and looked indignant. 'Nothing, nothing, nothing. We've told about fifteen policemen the same thing. We were told that the patient had a fear of needles. Well that's common enough. There was no call for a hypodermic syringe near the patient and I never saw one in the house. The doctor never needed one. I did suggest that he supplied us with one that we could use as a threat whenever the old... gentleman was playing us up but the doc knew I was half joking.'

'Only half?' said Grace.

'Perhaps two-thirds.'

She gave the nurses tea and sweet biscuits while she continued her questions, but she could think of little relevant to ask and so it was no surprise that she learned nothing else of interest. They left at last to go and settle in with Hilda Munro. They were hardly out of the door when Stuart made an appearance in the sitting room.

'You should have come through for a cup of tea,' Grace said.

'I was hiding in my study,' Stuart confessed. 'Tea and biscuits with a whole gang of women comes close to my idea of hell.'

'I am a woman,' Grace pointed out.

'I sometimes think,' said Stuart, 'that you are the only woman I really like. And possibly your mother, on a good day.'

'That's good,' Grace said. 'Let's keep it like that.'

They set about finalising the arrangement of the house, rather hampered by the fact that their ideas of what should go where were often diametrically opposed. Grace knew that whatever dispositions were made now would become rock-hard and permanent. She was stiffening up from her fall and the strain of lifting the urn one-handed. It was a relief when they were interrupted by another visitor.

Grace went to the door. The newcomer was a colourless man in a dark suit. He had a weak mouth only partly camouflaged by a moustache. 'Isaacson,' he said. 'Caledonian Building Society.'

'And my husband's uncle's executor,' Grace retorted, rather pleased with herself for making the connection so quickly. 'Do come in.'

Stuart met them in the hall. Grace let the two men have the sitting room to themselves but she heard them moving around the house while she began preparations for the evening meal.

The meal was ready before she heard the guest leaving. She breathed a sigh of relief. Any further delay and she would have been forced to invite Mr Isaacson to share their meal but two lamb chops would be impossible to share between three. She had just decided to defrost a sausage for herself when she heard voices at the front door and Stuart's footsteps, still with a slight limp, came along the hall. Grace took the plates out of the warm oven. 'Sit down and eat it before it spoils,' she told him. 'This is us, at last, in our own home, alone together and embarking on married life and I want to savour it even more than I want to know what you two found to talk about.'

Stuart washed, sat and began to eat. He took a sip of the red wine that Grace had brought. 'Yes,' he said simply.

When the first rush of hunger was satisfied, Grace said, 'All right. Tell me now. What did the executor say?'

'Not a lot.' Stuart filled his mouth once more, chewed and swallowed. 'He came through to inspect my uncle's personal chattels, or so he said, but after the doctor's had his whack it all comes to me anyway. The estate doesn't come within a million miles of being taxable and he surely couldn't think that the old man had enough valuables here to make up the difference. I think he was just being nosy.' Stuart finished clearing his plate.

'But what did he *say*?' Grace asked again.

'He didn't tell me any more about how the money came to be deposited. I don't think he ever even *met* my uncle except at the time when he was asked to act as executor.'

'Did he say when we'd get the money?' Grace got up to fetch the sweet course.

'He was a bit cagey about that. I don't think he wanted to say aloud that he couldn't distribute the estate as long as there was the possibility of one of the beneficiaries being implicated in the death. Why are you so concerned?'

'I know it's your money —'

'Don't think of it like that. It's ours.'

Grace put down a bowl of trifle with cream in front of him. She bent and kissed him on the ear. 'A thousand thanks,' she said. 'But what I was going to say is that the sitting room needs decoration and some fresh furniture.'

'Now that you mention it, I suppose it does. But I was rather hoping to get you a car,' Stuart said without looking up.

'You're a living doll – what are you?' Grace blinked away a tear of pure joy. 'Another thousand thanks!'

'As the Norwegians say, a hundred would be enough. Leave it with me. We'll see if we can't do both.' He raised his head and looked at her seriously. 'You do realise that if my uncle's death isn't explained soon, it could be a long while before we touch a penny?'

'I know that, I'm just not letting it spoil my mood. While we wait for that happy day, did you ask him if I could use your uncle's car?'

'I forgot. I'll phone him tomorrow. If you can bear to be seen in that old banger.'

'I must have wheels of some sort, living out here. Otherwise I'll have to rely on borrowing Geordie's motorbike when you're away at the school. When does the MOT on your uncle's car run out?'

An hour later they were interrupted again by the doorbell. A quick look through the sitting room window revealed a car waiting in the road. From the sign on the roof, Stuart recognised it as a taxi. In the far north of Scotland, where population density is at a minimum, anyone without their own motorised transport is considered seriously deprived and neither could think of anyone so handicapped who was likely to be paying a call. Stuart and Grace raised a pair of eyebrows – one apiece – and went to the door together.

Politely awaiting their answer, hat in hand, was a thickset man with a friendly yet businesslike expression on the slightly battered face of a Rugby-player or an amateur boxer. Even seen in half silhouette against the light outside, the striated skin and recession of his pepper-and-salt hair suggested that he was well into middle age but he carried himself with the upright posture of one who had seen military service. Stuart only noticed that he seemed well dressed but Grace who, having made professional stays in many different households, was in some respects more worldly-wise than her schoolteacher husband, recognised his shoes, suit and haberdashery as being of the very best. She had seen his tie before, thin stripes of different colours on a background of black, but which of the premier public schools it betokened evaded her for the moment.

His voice, when he wished them good morning, was pitched rather high for that of a man of such solid build. He had the neutral accent that has replaced the Establishment bray. He glanced round to satisfy himself that he was not overheard. 'I'm Desmond Carradine,' he said, 'and I'm personal secretary to Her Grace the Dowager Duchess Cecilia. I hope that I haven't called at a bad time but the matter has a certain urgency. May I come in for a few minutes?'

Grace had been half satisfied as to the nurses' innocence by their revelations about the delivery of the suppositories. Perhaps one absolution was enough for a single day. This arrival, strongly reminding her of the spurious equerry, raised immediate hackles of suspicion. On the other hand, would a fake be quite so well dressed? While she still hesitated, Stuart was quicker off the mark. 'What the hell are you?' he demanded. 'Media or another con artist?'

The visitor remained calm. He looked concerned but managed a simultaneous smile. 'I can assure you,' he said, 'that I'm neither of those.'

Grace decided that he could be exactly what he claimed to be but still be carrying a burden of guilt. 'You'd better come in,' she said. She led the way into the sitting room. She was relieved that she had turned the photograph to face the wall. 'Do you have any identification?' she asked.

He nodded. 'Very sensible of you,' he said. He produced a

security pass bearing his name and photograph and also a manu-
script letter on Oswald House paper. Grace and Stuart read it
together.

This is to introduce Desmond Carradine. He is my secretary and
has my full confidence. He is authorised to act for me in every mat-
ter. Please give him the fullest co-operation.

The small but round and looping handwriting was the same as
they had seen on the letters or a remarkably good forgery. Grace
noticed that it flowed without hesitation, showing no sign of the
stops and starts that betray a forgery. It was signed with the
Duchess's full name and titles.

'I'm satisfied,' Grace said. 'Please sit down, Mr Carradine. It is
Mister?'

'Mister will do very well.' Carradine sat, paying careful attention to his creases. Bonzo tried to climb onto his knee but was
gently removed to the floor. 'You've seen the letters?'

'We have,' Stuart said. 'They were dug up during some major
alterations to the garden here. We then realised for the first time
why my uncle had been so upset when he realised that the garden
was being remodelled.'

'Then you'll appreciate the great need for confidentiality. Any
kind of publicity would be very damaging to Her Grace, to the
present duke and, by adding to other recent scandals, to the
monarchy generally. From the tone of your greeting, I gather that
you've been contacted by other parties?'

'We have,' Grace said. She could have added that the other
party had probably been silenced, but until she was quite sure
how the land lay it might prove unwise to suggest that she and
Stuart were the only holders of the secret. 'How do you come to
be here?'

'A guarded approach reached us through a legal firm that
sometimes does work for us. Her Grace sent me immediately to
recover the letters.' His mouth twisted for a moment. 'Those letters should never have been written and, once written, should
have been burned on receipt,' he said hotly. When he spoke again
it was more mildly. 'But young people in love… And she was in
love. Your uncle must have been a remarkable man, because she's

usually a hard-headed woman and yet she loved him for many years. Believe me, she is a very tough old lady – I should know, because I handle most of her charitable work – but you can still see her melt when his name's mentioned. And he must have felt the same about her or he would have had the sense to burn them.' Carradine shrugged and looked from Grace to Stuart. 'I must know – to what extent is the secret breached?'

Grace was becoming satisfied but she still looked for more fragments of confirmation. 'For the moment, it's contained. You'll soon know if it gets out,' she said. 'What I meant by my question was, how did you get here?'

'I have my own plane.' His tone suggested that having one's own plane was a normal state of affairs. 'I flew to the airstrip at Dornoch and called a taxi. Now, who found the letters?'

'My wife did,' Stuart said.

'Who else has seen them?'

'The lawyer who attempted to contact you,' said Grace. 'One man who was present when I found them had a glimpse of one letter. He tried to come back and steal them but he failed and I think his mouth has been shut.'

It was only when Carradine began to relax that they could see how tense he had been. 'And how do I get them back?' he asked carefully.

'We are not asking money for them,' Stuart began.

His open nature was on the point of throwing away their only bargaining counter. Grace spoke quickly. 'Since the death, we have been subjected to suspicion. The police are investigating. Our acquaintances – I won't call them friends – are looking at us sideways. You can have the letters back, free and clear, as soon as we are sure that they bear no relationship to Mr Cameron's death.'

Mr Carradine raised a finger but was too polite to point it. 'Now I understand,' he said with satisfaction. 'We've met this sort of response in the past. The conspiracy theory. But why should Her Grace or anyone else want her lover killed?'

'Former lover. Because of his stroke,' said Grace. 'While he was alive and with all his faculties, he was no threat. Safely dead, the same. But after a stroke, he might have rambled. He might have talked to somebody who would sell the story to the media.'

Carradine still showed no anger at the supposition. 'I see,' he said thoughtfully. 'From your viewpoint, it has a certain logic. But I think I may be able to satisfy you. You see, until Mr Cameron was dead we knew nothing about his stroke. You knew that they still wrote to each other and met from time to time?'

'The letters that I saw weren't dated,' Stuart said. 'And on a weekday the post never comes until after I've left the house. If I ever saw one of her unopened letters during his lifetime I probably took it for one of those camouflaged charity appeals.'

'I see. The only news of him that ever reached her was by way of his letters. Despite the longstanding connection, there was no way that Her Grace would get to know about his stroke. In the case of some slower illness he would certainly have written to her. The first that we knew of his indisposition was when her last letter to him was returned.'

Stuart snapped his fingers, 'It came on the day he died. I took it for a piece of junk mail, just as I said. There was only a crest that I didn't recognise on the envelope but the Royal Mail is very clever at tracing addresses. I didn't suppose that it would matter a damn if it never got back. I just marked it "Return to sender" and put it back in the mail.'

'It came back to Oswald House,' said Carradine. He looked up at the ceiling, drew a deep breath and blew it out again. 'I nearly had kittens. You see, the Post Office had opened the letter. By the grace of God it was comparatively innocent, just expressing concern that the writer had not heard from him for some months and enquiring after his health and wellbeing. I telephoned here immediately and was told that he had died. A female voice.' He waited, eyebrows raised.

'My voice,' Grace said. 'In fact, I recognise yours now. I thought that there was something familiar about it when you first spoke.'

'Well, the return of that letter was the first we knew of his death. On Her Grace's instructions, I sent a wreath, anonymously. I may say that it seemed to knock the stuffing right out of her. Her grief still seems to outweigh any concern over the harm that revelation of her secrets could do. She would have attended the funeral if she could, but it was out of the question so, instead, she spent the day in private mourning. There seemed to be no more action to be taken just then. We rather hoped that the other letters would moulder away, unseen. Then we learned that they had been found.'

'All right,' said Grace. 'It seems to fit together. We'll accept for the moment that all that you've said is truth. But there is plenty of time for any discrepancies to come out. You see, the letters are safe in the custody of a solicitor and there they stay until any questions surrounding Mr Cameron's death are finally answered.'

'You really do believe that Mr Cameron may have been eliminated on the orders of somebody close to Her Grace,' Mr Carradine said wonderingly. 'But I assure you that she would never have countenanced any such action.'

'But would she necessarily have known?' Stuart asked. 'You seem to be taking the initiative in – if you'll forgive the expression – trying to scrape earth over the mess. There must be others in her entourage who might have had a lot to lose in the event of a scandal; power and prestige in particular. Can you vouch for the Duke?'

'I can assure you that nobody at our end knows about the affair, except for her maid and me. The Duke has been in New Zealand for the past month. He knows nothing.'

'Does he have any doubts about his parentage?'

For the first time, Mr Carradine looked alarmed. 'For God's sake, no! Don't whisper it aloud. Don't even *think* it. He isn't in the direct line of succession, in fact it would take a major calamity to bring him into line for the throne, but constitutional monarchy has provided us with one of the world's most stable societies and any more doubts of that nature could rock the whole structure.'

'If we were going to shout it aloud, we wouldn't have sent confidential messages to you over the legal network. Anyway,' Stuart said, 'try to see it from our point of view. Suspicion is floating around in search of somebody to stick to. My wife and my uncle had been at loggerheads. It appeared that she would have been saddled with the job of nursing a half-paralysed but obstreperous patient, perhaps for many years. That patient died by means strongly suggesting a degree of medical knowledge and access to unusual drugs. My wife was a nurse and is a physiotherapist. One more unfortunate coincidence and the police may decide to move against her. In that eventuality, we might be forced to produce the letters in order to show that others had the motivation and could certainly have commanded the expertise. I'm sorry, but that's the way it is.'

'And you would bring this disaster down on so many people, just to furnish a red herring?' Carradine sounded incredulous.

Stuart looked at him bleakly. 'To protect my wife, I would start World Wars Three, Four and Five.'

Gratifying as she found that statement, Grace felt the need to qualify it before Mr Carradine decided to call for drastic action by everyone from the SAS to Special Branch. 'It won't come to that,' she said. 'Stuart just wants you to understand that we can't let our last line of defence go out of our hands until the danger's past. How can we get in touch with you?'

'I shall not be far away. Can you recommend a good hotel?'

'Canmore House,' Grace said. 'Straight across the Firth. You can almost see it from here.'

'I shall put up there for a few days. Please keep in touch. We may even be able to help. It is in everybody's interest – yours, ours and the national interest – that the death of Mr Cameron be solved quickly and without any need to spill secrets. In fact, there is a very reputable firm of private detectives we sometimes use for confidential business. If their services might help, you only have to say the word.'

'Just at the moment,' Grace said, 'I don't think they would. But we'll bear the offer in mind.'

Grace slept badly, waking and sleeping by turns. Too many possible permutations of events past and those still to come were fizzing around in her brain. She snapped awake early, to a series of aches from her bruised back and also in her right arm, which latter she knew derived from the jerk and strain when she had lifted the urn, one-handed, through two vehicle windows. It had, she decided, been worth it. Nevertheless, she had no intention of letting her fitness go to waste. She resumed her old habit of a morning run up the hill, among the forestry plantations, followed by her hot shower. Her muscles began to loosen up and were almost back to normal after she had worked over her right arm and shoulder with the electric vibrator.

Stuart decided to resolve his dispute with the school secretary by a morning visit. He would return, he promised, before there was time for any fresh dramas to develop. His car had hardly vanished along the road, however, before Detective Inspector Fauldhouse made an appearance. Grace realised later that the Inspector must have been lurking nearby in the hope of catching her as soon as she was alone. He was accompanied by Sergeant Ballintore.

Grace's first inclination was to tell the Inspector to go and bowl his hoop. But she had a sense of wellbeing after her exercise and shower and, although her knowledge of the law was fragmentary, she was fairy sure that the Inspector would be within his powers if he carried her off for inquisition at the nearest police station, leaving the breakfast dishes unwashed, the puppy unfed and the bed unmade.

She escorted the two policemen into the sitting room and pointed out seats, only then realising that Stuart, in an excess of mischief which had already outlived its power to entertain, had unearthed the photograph from her hiding-place behind the chest of drawers and replaced it on the mantelpiece. During the ensuing debate she was distracted by her efforts to keep their attention from it by eye contact and willpower. Bonzo tried to find a friend, failed and wandered, disgusted, to the kitchen where she was sure that breakfast would appear sooner or later.

Inspector Fauldhouse plunged in immediately. 'Mrs Campbell, you admit to having done hospital nursing.'

Grace was not going to let him away with that. 'It's not an admission, Inspector. I'm proud of it.'

The Inspector let Grace score the point. 'In hospitals and elsewhere in the medical professions, are drugs strictly controlled?'

There would be no point in trying to hide what he must have been told by other sources. 'There are systems and checks. They can never be a hundred per cent effective.' It had been some time since she had left nursing for physiotherapy. Grace cast her mind back, at the same time arranging her recollections into a tidy statement that could leave no room for misinterpretation or editing. 'The issue and recovery of drugs is made the responsibility of a person or office. That is usually effective when ampoules or tablets are issued and a set number can be counted out and back, though even that isn't infallible. It may happen, for instance, that by the time the nurse reaches the patient the doctor has changed the medication or the patient may even have died or been removed for surgery. In some departments it's even more difficult, because quantities of liquid or powder will be much more difficult to check. An anaesthetist, for instance, goes on feeding in anaesthetic by injection until the patient goes under. Many anaesthetists proceed by having the patient count downwards and when the patient stops counting, that's it. The anaesthetist later feeds in an antidote until the patient can be seen to be waking up again. Those are not fixed quantities and nobody could possibly check that any quantity returned to the store were correct.'

'And that would apply to Scoline?'

'I'd certainly suppose so. I do know that the stomach muscles in particular sometime stay active. I would expect the anaesthetist to inject Scoline, up to a measured maximum, until the muscles became still.'

'So you're saying that in a hospital, or even a medical practice, there could be drugs unaccounted for?'

'That's what I did say, Inspector.'

'Have you ever had any such controlled drugs in your personal possession?'

'No, never.'

The Inspector treated her to what he no doubt believed to be a piercing look and changed his line of attack. 'Mrs Campbell, you did private nursing before you studied physiotherapy?'

'Yes.'

'Did any of your patients die?'

Grace remembered the argument put to her only the previous day. 'Yes, of course they did. That's in the nature of the job. Sometimes a nurse is called in to look after somebody while they recover from illness or injury. Occasionally that person won't make it. But at other times, the patient's illness is terminal. The family respects their wish to die at home and not among strangers. Nurses get used to it. Death is part of their life.'

'Patients are grateful?'

'Sometimes. Some are resentful, as if their aches and pains were the nurse's fault, but some are almost pathetically grateful.'

'Did any of your patients mention you in their wills?'

'Yes.'

The Inspector seemed to be caught flat-footed by the straight-forward reply. He hesitated before asking, 'How many?'

'I don't know,' Grace said. She was taking a perverse pleasure in leading the Inspector up blind alleys. 'Several of the few that I knew about are still alive. They've almost certainly changed their wills again by now.'

'I'll rephrase the question,' the Inspector said patiently. 'Did you ever receive a bequest from a patient?'

'Only once. An old lady left me a coral necklace. She was a nice old dear and though it was of no particular value it was a pretty thing and I treasured it. It got lost. I think that a colleague borrowed it and forgot to return it.'

The Inspector glanced at Detective Sergeant Ballintore's moving pencil and at the slowly rotating reels of the little tape recorder. 'And did a patient ever give you a present? A patient, I mean, who subsequently died.'

'Of course,' Grace said. 'But never anything of any value.'

'Can you furnish me with a list of such presents?'

'Above what value?'

'All presents.'

'No,' Grace said. 'I will not. I couldn't. Consider for a moment. A patient gives me a box of chocolates. A day or two later I bring the patient some fruit. We share both the fruit and the chocolates. Even if I could remember such exchanges, how could I estimate the difference in values? And what use would the information be to you? Anyway, any accidental omissions would be regarded as guilty suppressions.'

'Very well, then. Gifts to a value of more than, say, ten pounds.'

'That's easy. Inspector. None whatever.'

'Will you furnish me with a list of patients whom you nursed privately?

'Again, no.'

'You force me to consult the agency you used to work for and then go to the families of the deceased.' The Inspector leaned forward. Any attempt to hold Grace's eye was frustrated by the fact that she was already holding his. 'Mrs Campbell, have you ever committed an act of euthanasia?'

'Certainly not.'

'Mrs Campbell, I see that orders will have to be obtained for the exhumation of several of your late patients.'

Grace was beginning to shake with anger. She got to her feet. 'Inspector, I am not answering any more of your very suggestive questions except in the presence of my solicitor. Please go.'

To her surprise, the two policemen rose. Grace moved quickly in front of the photograph. She pointed to the door. When they were out, she turned the photograph to face the wall again. As soon as she could find where Stuart had hidden the negative she must destroy both, but for the moment he was too clever for her. The school held an annual photography competition. On the principle of 'if you can't hide it make a feature of it', she thought of putting in the photograph as the entry of the depute headmaster. That, when he set eyes on it, would wipe the silly smirk off his face.

She phoned Mr McCormick's number but the solicitor was out

of the office, possibly for the remainder of the day. Grace left a message asking him to call her.

She referred to the directory to find a number for Molly Grange. That young lady, she knew, had a constitutional aversion to work. If cash in hand plus any benefit that she could coax out of the Welfare State sufficed for the moment to maintain her modest lifestyle, she might well be found at home and probably still in bed. Sure enough, a sleepy voice answered on the eighth ring.

'Molly, it's Grace. You were good enough to warn me that people were saying I'd poisoned Mr Cameron.'

The sound of a huge yawn came over the wire. 'There's still talk. But they've stopped talking about whether you did it, they're wondering how you did it. It seems to be taken for granted that you did.'

'I didn't, but I don't suppose they'll accept that until the police do.' Grace paused. It is a quirk of human intercourse that the subject of gossip is very often unaware of it. 'Perhaps it's your turn for gossip. You seemed very sure that Dr Sullivan was out of the country at the crucial time. Are they saying that you went off on holiday with Dr Sullivan?'

There was another pause. 'I can't honestly say that I'm surprised,' Molly said. 'After all, it's the truth.' She sounded defensive. The Highland attitude to morality is mixed. Promiscuity is deeply shocking whereas a faithful, longstanding relationship prior to marriage is quite understood. 'Why shouldn't I enjoy a week in Barbados with a clean and well-mannered man who isn't very demanding? If it wasn't me it would have been somebody else, probably Emmaline Braid. And after all, if you can't trust a doctor to practise safe sex, who can you trust?'

Grace was not going to be drawn into a discussion of doctoral hygiene. 'You came back together?' she asked. 'Which day did you get back?'

Molly looked in her diary – Grace heard the pages turning – and quoted a date. Dr Sullivan had quite definitely been out of the country in the period during which the suppositories might have been doctored.

Grace put the phone down, frowning. The doctor seemed to be exonerated. The nurses were extremely unlikely suspects. She knew that she had not killed her uncle by marriage and she thought that she could be sure of Stuart. Who had she forgotten? She could not think of anybody local. That left Mr Carradine and his colleagues. A mere assurance that the stroke had never come to their attention was hardly sufficient. The Dowager might still have been nursing a fondness for Duncan Cameron, but if Stuart's uncle was seen as a threat to their comfortable lives, somebody in her entourage might well have decided to take pre-emptive action. But how would they have gone about it? How would they even have known that suppositories were prescribed? Given that a few handsome bribes might procure that sort of information, what then? The possibility of corruption and tampering might exist at any point along the line – the wholesalers, the post office, the nurses – but proof would not only be lacking but inaccessible.

What courses were open to her? She could, of course, play a waiting game… during which rumour would continue to sprout and the Inspector would continue to build a case against her. But – Holy Hell! – just suppose that the family of one of her early patients had committed euthanasia. One… or more. The consequences could be unthinkable. Instead, she could blow the whistle now and rock the Establishment as it had seldom been rocked, giving the Inspector something else to worry about. Or there was the median course. She could explain to Mr Carradine that she was being harassed and threatened and might have to reveal all. Surely there must be somebody accessible to the dowager's retinue who could bring the Inspector to heel. Or she might take up his offer of the services of a discreet and efficient detective agency.

She must consult Mr McCormick. But where would his loyalties lie? If he happened to be an ardent monarchist, would that outweigh his loyalty to a client?

It seemed that she was about to be given her chance to find out. Mr McCormick's Shogun, black over silver, was pulling into the driveway. The solicitor, it seemed, had the knack of materialising as if summoned by a single thought. Wondering what to say, she went out to meet him.

For the first time since she had met him, the solicitor was showing animation. Grace thought herself good at reading faces and body language but she could not decide whether he was pleased or anxious – perhaps, she thought, a little of each. As she invited him in, she noticed that Bonzo was playing with a folded sheet of brown paper on the hall floor. With the house pristine for the moment, she could do without shredded paper all over the hall. She lifted it absently and took the puppy under her other arm.

'I have news,' the solicitor said. 'I think perhaps you'd better sit down.' He remained standing. He glanced at the mantelpiece and seemed disappointed that the photograph was not on view.

Grace did not consider herself to be the sort of person who would fold at the knees when surprised, but she sat down anyway while nodding the solicitor to the opposite chair. Was this to be some disastrous tidings?

Apparently not. 'We seem to be making progress,' Mr McCormick said. 'The client I was representing in the sheriff court suddenly decided to plead guilty – which, I may say, I had been begging him to do since Day One. Finding myself free, I phoned the office and was given your message. At the same time, my apprentice, who was doing the phoning for me, gave me some very interesting data. He has some very useful contacts and was making full use of them. Would you care to speak first? What did you want to discuss?'

Rather than waste more time in argument, Grace acceded. 'Detective Inspector Fauldhouse was here, not long ago. He seems to have convinced himself that I murdered my husband's uncle and he proposes to dig up some of my previous patients to discover whether any of them died unnatural deaths.'

'Probably an idle threat, intended to unbalance you.'

'But possibly not. And suppose that one or more of them really was put to sleep by a well meaning relative! Thinking back, there were one or two that I'm none too happy about.'

'I take your point and, anyway, such activities would undoubtedly be picked up by the media and you would be tainted for life or until another arrest was made, whichever came first.'

'It could be more serious than that,' Grace said. She spoke slowly. By voicing her troubles she felt that she might be making them more real. 'I've been avoiding telling anyone about this but now I think I must. Almost the last patient that I had before going over to physiotherapy had been a successful writer. He had Alzheimer's disease. The loss of his mental faculties distressed him enormously. He felt that whatever he had ever been had gone down the drain. His wife adored him and she was near suicide at his distress. His sister-in-law was a hospital pharmacist. I was suspicious at the time and now I'm almost certain. Do I need to say any more?'

Mr McCormick managed not to show any emotion but the effort of doing so was detectable. 'No, I don't think you do. If it should be the case that your patient was relieved of a burdensome life by one of his family, it could be made to appear very black for you, and I don't see the family rushing to exonerate you. So we had better move with all possible dispatch. Happily, there has been a turn in our favour at last. I'll give you my news. Unless the doctor is as much plagued by coincidences as you are, he is not the paragon of virtue that he is believed to be.'

Grace was disappointed. Was this the big news? 'I don't think that anyone believes him to be a paragon of virtue,' she pointed out. 'As far as I know, he doesn't mess with his women patients though it's said that he enjoys examining them rather more than he properly should. But his carrying-on with other ladies, some of them quite young, is a byword.'

'Be that as it may,' said the solicitor, 'I was not referring to the vigour which I hope that I may be able to emulate at his age and which I have known about for years. It transpires that my office has so far found no less than four patients who have died within the last three years after making wills that included legacies to Doctor Sullivan. That, while not yet in the class of some of his predecessors in medical serial murder – Bodkin Adams and Harold Shipman spring to mind, but there have been others – is far enough above the national average to suggest something seriously amiss.'

'Whether or not something is amiss,' Grace said, 'I understand that the suppositories were sent direct from the wholesaler while the doctor was abroad with one of his popsies. And I was present, remember, when Mr Cameron died. The doctor had only just arrived at the house. He had examined the patient but, as I recall it, he had had no opportunity to substitute suppositories. And I couldn't say anything different on oath even to save myself.'

'Perhaps on a previous visit…?'

'We can ask the questions but I'm sure that it was his first visit since his return from abroad. He was somewhere in the Caribbean with a friend of the female persuasion,' Grace felt the need to speak lightly, laughing that she might not weep, 'for the period when the suppositories would have been delivered.'

Having uncovered such a strong pointer, the solicitor was not readily going to abandon the doctor as a suspect. 'That might not matter. He might have had an accomplice.'

'In murder?'

'It's possible. Even an unknowing one. Let's think about it.' Mr McCormick thought for several minutes. Grace was not impressed but decided against speaking in case the solicitor might come up with some clever piece of reasoning that she had missed. In the end, Mr McCormick sighed. 'I'm afraid not,' he said. 'I would like to envisage the doctor leaving for his jolly week in the Caribbean and telling one of his partners or his receptionist to doctor or substitute the suppositories when they are delivered and post them here, but I can not think of a single plausible reason that he could give for such an action. Except for money, of course, but his legacy would hardly be enough to share and still be a sufficient inducement. Unless, of course, there's some factor that we know nothing about.'

Grace had dumped Bonzo on the floor, resisting all the puppy's efforts to return to the warmth and comfort of a lap. While she spoke, Grace had been smoothing over her knee the brown paper from just inside the front door. She remembered Alicia's promise. 'This seems to be the paper the suppository box was wrapped in,' she said. 'Alicia, one of the nurses, told me that she still had it and I asked her to put it through the door.'

'Let me see. No,' he added quickly as she made to hand it to him, 'let's not add any more fingerprints. Lay it down on the coffee table.' She did as he suggested and they both studied the paper.

'It's been tampered with,' Grace said. She got to her feet and held the paper against the window glass. With the bright light behind it, the printing beneath showed clearly. 'This was posted to the surgery,' she said. 'It was supposed to be sent here but the wholesaler was probably afraid of breaking the law. Somebody then made a label on a computer, giving the address of this house and then stuck it over the old label, just leaving the supplier's address showing at the bottom. And they steamed off the old stamps and stuck new ones on. The paper's wrinkled and a bit of the old postmark's still showing.'

The solicitor had been studying the paper even more closely. 'What's more, the scotch tape had been slit with a razor blade or something equally sharp. Somebody tried very hard to tape it again, matching up the new tape with the old, but that isn't as easy to do as you might think.'

'This brings something else back to my mind,' Grace said. 'Just after Mr Cameron died, the doctor muttered something about always feeling guilty.'

Mr McCormick raised his eyebrows. 'That could be perfectly innocent but a jury might give it some weight. Did anybody else hear him say that?'

'Not so far as I remember. But surely,' Grace said, 'this paper lets me off the hook? The original address is under the new label. Nobody would believe that I could have faked all this.'

'The allegation might be made. And how do we prove that this is the original wrapping paper? The chain of evidence is seriously incomplete.'

'Inspector Fauldhouse should be able to turn up the missing bits of evidence.'

'Doubtful.' Grace began to wonder again whose side the solicitor was on. Mr McCormick seated himself and stared at the ceiling in silent contemplation for some seconds. 'I'm sure,' he said at last, 'that the Inspector is a perfectly worthy policeman but I do not think that we will hand over this paper until it has been seen by several reputable witnesses and also photographed. Some policemen whose acquaintance I have reluctantly made – on behalf of my clients, I may add – would have filed it away rather than do a lot of work to discredit their own case. I also think that we need to know as much about Doctor Sullivan as we can possibly find out, before we approach Inspector Fauldhouse again.'

'And how do we do that?' Grace asked.

'We go to see him, of course, but with a good cover. Let's see now. We are considering taking proceedings against him. His professional negligence permitted Mr Cameron's death and the doctor thereafter certified the death as being natural. The result was that the funeral had to be interrupted with the consequent effect that rumour circulated about you, to your great distress and financial loss.'

'That wouldn't stand up in court for a minute, would it?'

'It doesn't have to stand up in court,' Mr McCormick said impatiently. 'But it's quite good enough to let us call for a precognition and ask a lot of very pointed questions about the doctor's treatment of his patient and the relationship between them. Do you have a car?'

'I have the use of Mr Cameron's old car. The executor,' Grace explained, 'has been avoiding us like the plague. I suppose that that's in case we turn out to be guilty. He wouldn't want to have handed out a legacy to the guilty party. But the car's only worth scrap value, so when Stuart phoned him he agreed to my using it until we have our affairs sorted out, after which I can trade it in for a car of my own. It should get me as far as the surgery and possibly even back again, if that's what you're suggesting.'

'That's exactly what I had in mind,' Mr McCormick said. 'You can follow me. It will save me having to come all the way back round the Firth after we've finished and I'll be able to hurry straight back to the office and process anything that we may have discovered. In the meantime, I don't want to disturb any of the folds in this paper. Your fingerprints are already on it. Perhaps you would carry it out to my car by the edges and lay it flat on the back seat where we can cover it with my coat?'

'Yes, of course.'

Bonzo, it transpired, had retired to the kitchen in a huff and there had made a mess on the floor. It went against the grain to leave it, but Mr McCormick was waiting. Grace compromised by giving the puppy a little shake, dropping her into her sandbox and putting a newspaper over the puddle. It would be good practice, she told herself, for when family began to arrive.

Chapter Seventeen

The VW Polo belonging to the late Mr Cameron had been soundly constructed, but that had been some years earlier. Grace was not very knowledgeable about cars in general or Volkswagens in particular, but she was fairly sure that there should not be quite so many noises coming from so many different places. Even an air-cooled engine, she thought, lacking the sound absorption of a water-jacket, should not release quite so much noise of tappets and bearings. The car was, she thought, capable of conveying her from place to place and not a lot more, but at least the seats were clean and it responded adequately to movements of the steering wheel.

Once they were on the move, Mr McCormick pulled away but he soon noticed that Grace was having difficulty matching his pace and lowered his speed. On the journey, therefore, Alice had time to reflect that if the suppositories had passed through the surgery, presumably being tampered with *en route*, the doctor must have had a conspirator among his colleagues. Or else he had broken his holiday for a quick flight back. But with Concorde no longer flying and all the delays built into air travel in the interests of anti-terrorism, economy and the convenience of the airline operators, plus the need to leave no back-trail, that would have taken a huge bite out of a week's holiday. She wished now that she had asked Molly Grange the specific question; but once the likelihood of conspiracies was accepted the possibilities proliferated endlessly without any certainly of an honest answer.

Come to think of it, she had only Molly's word as to the dates on which the holiday had started and finished. She thought that she could trust Molly; but nobody had so far shown any connection with Stuart's uncle who she would not have considered wholly trustworthy. Which, she supposed, marked her as naively gullible and trusting. Well, better that than living in perpetual suspicion of her fellows. She hoped that her trust in her fellow men was not being permanently distorted.

She caught up with Mr McCormick as the automatic doors of the surgery hissed open. The car park was almost empty. Miss

Dawburn, who they found reigning in solitary state over a nearly empty waiting room, explained that Dr Sullivan was out on a call, Dr Mearns had left for his holiday as soon as Dr Sullivan had returned and Dr Broch had had a late surgery the previous evening but was due to come in and start another surgery in an hour's time. For the moment, the only activity in the building was that of the practice nurse, inoculating babies and bandaging septic toes.

In her innocence, Grace would have apologised and made an appointment for later in the day. She was not prepared for the deviousness of the legal mind. 'I wonder if I might take a seat in your waiting room for a few minutes,' Mr McCormick said faintly. 'I seem to be starting one of my migraines. They never last very long if I just can sit still and quiet.' He laid a little emphasis on the last word while looking doubtfully at a howling baby in the waiting room.

Miss Dawburn took the hint. She invited them through the glass screen into the office, gave them chairs, provided Mr McCormick with a glass of water and offered to fetch him an ibuprofen from the drugs cupboard that stood in the corner beside a padlocked refrigerator.

Grace caught a meaning look from him and interpreted it correctly. 'You're in charge of the keys of the drugs cupboard, are you?' she asked admiringly. 'That must be quite a responsibility.'

Miss Dawburn was still on her feet. She had seen fit to come to work that day in a thin dress well provided with frills and flounces. The youthfulness of the dress had looked cruelly unsuitable, but it sat well with her suddenly coy expression. 'Not really,' she said. 'Dr Sullivan —' (Grace had the impression that she barely restrained herself from curtseying at the name) '- takes personal responsibility.' She paused. Grace thought that she was hesitating to admit what everybody knew, that the system was far from watertight. Miss Dawburn made up her mind. 'But life would be impossible if the other doctors couldn't dispense a prescription to some old dear, or the nurse couldn't collect a vaccine while Dr Sullivan was out, so the keys are kept in here.'

Which, Grace thought, negated the point of having a lockfast drugs cupboard at all.

'Surely,' said Mr McCormick, 'you wouldn't keep many drugs here?'

'No, not an awful lot; but we have to be prepared.' Miss Dawburn settled in a chair, prepared for a cosy chat. 'This is a rural practice, there isn't a pharmacist handy and we can't all drive cars, you know. Some of the old folk can hardly make it to the surgery without then having to find a way of getting to the chemist and back, so we have a license to dispense. And we do have emergencies – road accidents or out on the farms or in the forestry or on the hills. Dr Sullivan goes out with the Mountain Rescue, I think that's what keeps him so fit. It takes time for an ambulance or a helicopter to get here. If there's snow or fog, we can't count on outside help at all, so the doctors may have to do quite a lot of work here.'

Grace and Mr McCormick exchanged a look. 'Not surgery, surely,' Grace said.

'We don't have an operating theatre as such,' Miss Dawburn said regretfully. 'But there's a small room that we keep sterile and use for that purpose. We're not equipped for major surgery here but in a real emergency we can do all that's needed to keep the patient alive and save any damaged limbs until he can be trans-ferred to Inverness. We've several times had compliments from Raigmore about the work done here.'

'It must be a far cry from an Inverness practice,' Mr McCormick said. 'Who orders replacements when supplies get depleted?'

'Dr Sullivan leaves a note for me and I order what we need.'

Grace struggled to keep any sign of excitement out of her face. 'And there are only three doctors? How do you manage when one of them goes on holiday?'

'We get in a locum if he's needed.'

'Oh? Anybody I'd know?' Grace asked quickly.

'Probably, Miss Gillespie. Mrs Campbell, I should say. Do you remember Dr Gray? He only retired from this practice two years ago and he still stands in whenever he's needed.'

Miss Dawburn got up to attend to a lady who was hoping for

the results of a blood test. Grace and Mr McCormick exchanged facial signals and telepathic messages behind her back. Grace thought that Dr Gray might be a useful source of confirmation of Dr Sullivan's holiday dates.

'Only the doctors can give out that sort of information,' Miss Dawburn was saying. 'Shall I ask Dr Sullivan to phone you?' She lowered her voice to a whisper. 'Between ourselves, I think you can stop worrying.' The lady left. Miss Dawburn resumed her seat. 'What were we saying?' she asked.

'About locums,' Grace said. 'Yes, I remember Dr Gray very well. He still has a daughter at university, hasn't he? A university education's getting more and more expensive. I should think he finds the extra money very useful.'

'Not this time,' Miss Dawburn said, with a hint of malicious pleasure. 'We've been very quiet, so he's never had to come in at all.'

Grace had been hoping for news of a locum who might have been got at by the dowager's minions, but apparently it was not to be. 'His daughter's doing medicine, isn't she?'

'Yes, at Glasgow. She's been promised a place in the partnership when Dr Sullivan retires.'

Again Grace met Mr McCormick's eye. She hoped that she was reading him correctly, but he seemed to be urging her to follow up this hint. Idle gossip, his eye seemed to be saying, was more a woman's habit than a man's. 'When does Dr Sullivan plan to retire?' she asked. The solicitor relaxed visibly, so she knew that she had interpreted him correctly.

'He's always planned to go at the end of next year,' Miss Dawburn said. 'I don't think that that's changed.'

'He'll be missed.'

'Oh, I know.' Miss Dawburn spoke with an enthusiasm that had been absent from her idle chatter. 'Most of the patients ask for him personally. The younger doctors may know all the latest techniques and fads but I always say that there's no substitute for experience. And his manner is always just right, so friendly and yet so professional.'

Over Miss Dawburn's shoulder and through two glass doors,

Grace saw a car arriving which she was fairly sure was that of Dr Sullivan. If their time with Miss Dawburn at her most garrulous was running out, she would have to make the pace. She leaned forward and lowered her voice, girl to girl. (Mr McCormick leaned back and kept very still, striving for invisibility.) Grace said softly, 'I'm surprised that Dr Sullivan can afford to take early retirement, after that divorce.'

'That needn't hold up his plans.'

Mr McCormick was surprised enough to re-enter the discussion. 'Come now, Miss Dawburn,' he said in his best coaxing-a-witness manner. 'Fighting a divorce doesn't come cheap, especially if you're rash enough to engage the services of a top advocate from Edinburgh. The facts spoke for themselves. The good doctor was gambling that a really good counsel would earn his fee when their worldly goods were apportioned out, but according to the figures that were being bandied about, she received an enormous settlement and all that his expensive advocate gained him was a thumping legal bill on top of everything else.'

Miss Dawburn's eyes seemed ready to fill with tears. 'That was just awful,' she said. 'The poor doctor hardly slept for weeks after the judgement. That awful wife of his! And it was the purest spite. It's not as if she needed the money, her father left her well provided for and she's married again already. It used to make me furious to see her swanking around in a brand new Jaguar while he had to sign a hire purchase agreement before he could change his car. But that's all behind us now,' she added more cheerfully. 'Provision has been made.'

Grace noted the plural and, glancing at the solicitor, saw that he had registered it too. Once again, Grace could detect the tone of hero worship flavoured with a taste of motherly pride. Inspiration visited her with a stunning suddenness, as if a kaleidoscope had been shaken and the pattern had suddenly turned into one of unmistakable significance. How, she wondered, could she possibly have failed to see it earlier? It was blindingly obvious, almost a cliché – the middle aged spinster falling for her boss. Was she the last to recognise the signs?

The discussion, coming close as it did to matters of finance and business, seemed to Grace to be falling within his court rather than hers and she gave him a meaning look. Mr McCormick returned an almost imperceptible nod. 'The doctor's been lucky with his investments, has he?' he suggested.

The receptionist hesitated. Grace wondered whether they had come too close and made her wary. The office was so silent that Grace could hear the nurse's voice, at the other end of the corridor, soothing the now silent infant. 'You could say that,' Miss Dawburn said doubtfully at last.

'Well,' Grace said, 'something must have happened. He does have some rather expensive hobbies.'

Miss Dawburn bridled. 'Not really. He doesn't golf or drink or gamble. If you're thinking of his holidays, a busy doctor is surely entitled to a trip to the sunshine now and again.'

There was only one way to go from here or they could circle for ever. Perhaps it was too soon for shock tactics but the moment might never come again. Perhaps nobody had been so crass as to open up the subject directly with Miss Dawburn. So it was left to Grace to drop the bomb. But which attitude to pretend? Amused tolerance? Disapproval? Salacious curiosity? Romantic envy? Grace decided to be bluntly non-committal. 'The holidays are all right,' she said bluntly. 'As you say, a busy doctor needs to unwind now and again, but I would have thought that taking one of the local popsies along with him each time would double the cost. More than double it, in fact, because two people together always seem to do more than the same two people singly.'

Grace had hoped to provoke some reaction, but the result far exceeded her expectations. Miss Dawburn drew in a scandalised breath and her face burned. 'That's just horrible, local gossip,' she burst out. She jumped to her feet and then sat down again. 'You mustn't believe a word of it. I certainly don't.' She began wringing her hands, slowly at first and then faster and faster. 'People say the most awful things. You should hear what they're saying about you,' she finished with a razor's edge of spite in her voice.

'What are they saying about me?' Grace asked gently.

'That you killed Mr Campbell's uncle somehow, though I can't imagine how.' Was there or was there not a hint of a secret smile. 'I'm only the receptionist, I don't know anything about medicines and all like that, but they say that nurses have the knowledge and they deal with poisons every day. I don't believe any of that, so you see you mustn't believe anything you hear about the doctor.'

'You were a nurse too,' Grace said. 'I remember you at the school.'

Miss Dawburn twitched. 'That was... it was some time ago, dear, and I've forgotten all that I ever knew. And I know that there's no truth in what they're saying about you. Or about the dear doctor.'

How to twist the knife? 'I'm sure his motives are of the best,' Grace said. 'Perhaps he feels that some of these young people are underprivileged and need his help towards a holiday in the sun,' she suggested.

'But... but there's no truth in any of it,' Miss Dawburn protested. 'Not a word. He told me so himself. And he wouldn't lie to me. I know he wouldn't.' Behind her back, Dr Sullivan was approaching the counter on silent feet. Grace, with awful clarity, could see just where they were heading and she was powerless either to stop it or to hurry it along. It seemed that the world was waiting with bated breath.

Miss Dawburn's voice had risen still higher. There was a wild look in her eye. She made up her mind and rushed in. 'Dr Sullivan wouldn't lie to me. Don't say anything, because it's supposed to be a secret, but we... we're going to be married as soon as he retires. *There!*'

Into the silence crashed the doctor's footsteps as he came off the carpet onto tiles, followed by the rattle of the door handle and the click of the latch as he pushed the office door to behind him. Miss Dawburn's face took on the guilty look of children caught playing doctors and nurses.

The doctor glanced at Grace and Mr McCormick and when he spoke it was clearly at least half to the visitors. Despite the trying circumstances he had kept his composure and Grace had to admire his calm handling of a delicate quandary. 'My dear Miss

Dawburn,' he said kindly, 'you know that I have a high regard for you, but I can't have you putting it about that we're a couple. You have always put me, quite undeservedly, on a pedestal and I value your help in the practice enormously, but I've tried to explain to you before now that there has never been any question of marriage. I tried to put it as gently as I could, but perhaps I should have been more forceful.'

Miss Dawburn's face went from red to white and her nostrils seemed to flare. 'I'm glad this is out in the open at last,' she said. Her voice rose. 'It has never needed to be said aloud. There was an unspoken agreement. You know there was. There was no need for words or for anything physical. We've gone past the touchy-feely age. It needed only a glance, a change of tone, and we each knew what the other was thinking.'

'I thought we did but it seems that I was wrong,' said the doctor. He braced himself but when he spoke again it was in the gentle manner of a doctor with a frightened patient. 'Miss Dawburn, if I have led you, by word or deed, to imagine that there could ever be anything of a romantic nature between us, it was quite unintentional and I am truly sorry. I intend to enjoy my retirement, but that does not mean that I have the least intention of marrying again.'

'You can't mean it!'

'Please believe that I do mean it. I have the friendliest feelings toward you and I hope that we can go on working together until my retirement.'

His receptionist's voice was rising further in pitch, almost to a squeak. 'After all that we've been to each other!'

The doctor sighed. He had Grace's sympathy. She had once been the target of a one-sided devotion and she knew how fine a line lay between cruelty and *laissez-faire*. She saw him lift his chin and knew that he was making up his mind to be firm. 'I have never given you reason to believe that you were more to me than a valued colleague and a good friend,' he said. 'As for having been anything to each other, it remains as it always has been, out of the question.'

Miss Dawburn's face was working. Her voice had gone back to

a whisper but it stopped the doctor in mid sentence. 'You're despicable,' she muttered.

'Perhaps. I hope not,' said the doctor sadly.

'When I think what you owe me...'

'I owe you a great deal. You've been a support and a mainstay of this practice almost since I started it. We could never have managed without you. And I hope that you'll go on giving my partners your support after I've gone into my retirement.'

'Your retirement! It's only thanks to me that you can afford to retire,' she said. She had quite forgotten that they had any audience. There was spittle on her chin. Grace thought that she had progressed very quickly through the classic stage of denial into anger. There could be no doubt that the sudden damage to her fantasy had pushed the other woman over an edge.

Mr McCormick was leaning forward with a glint in his eye. Grace's mind hesitated to accept what she was hearing even though she was expecting it, but Doctor Sullivan understood. It was his turn to disbelieve. 'I don't know what you... Oh my God! You can't mean... Old Miss Glenn?' The doctor leaned back against the door and closed his eyes. 'No! My God, what have you done to me?'

'And Mr Watson,' Miss Dawburn said proudly. 'And Jemima Pruitt. And, of course, Mr Cameron. And the others – I've forgotten some of them. It was easy. I just had to drop a little hint that the rewards for a country doctor were a very poor return after giving so much to so many. Mr Watson hasn't gone yet – he gets his medication from the pharmacy in Bonar Bridge – but he won't live for ever.'

'The others,' said the doctor. 'You tampered with their medications?'

'They were old and suffering. They were already knocking on death's door. It was a merciful release for each of them, what they call an act of love. So, you see, you've got to marry me now. I've made you rich.' She began to laugh. It was a triumphant laugh but it was also very mad. Grace felt an atavistic shiver up her back but steeled herself to ignore it.

The doctor had gone very white. He opened his mouth but

could find nothing to say.

Grace slipped quietly out of the office and went to find the practice nurse. She found that lady tidying up after the last infant. 'You'd better come quickly,' Grace said. 'It's Miss Dawburn. I think she's heading for a nervous breakdown.'

The nurse was a tough and competent woman with a square jaw in a skull-like face. She was quite capable of restraining a terrified teenager or ejecting a farmer who wanted to interfere with his wife's treatment. She listened for a moment. The sound of hysteria penetrated the quiet room. 'Coming,' she said. 'It's not unexpected. She's been living a dream and it was bound to end in a tearful awakening some time.'

Grace followed the stiff, starched back along the hall, thinking that the nurse had no call to sound so pleased with herself. If she had voiced her suspicions earlier, she could have saved a lot of people a lot of grief. She might even have saved a few lives.

Miss Dawburn was sedated and settled in a vacant consulting room with the nurse on guard. Mr McCormick drew Grace aside. 'I must get hold of Inspector Fauldhouse quickly,' he said, 'while people are still in a talking mood. I'll phone from my car. You had better wait to make a statement.'

'I couldn't leave anyway,' Grace said. 'Dr Sullivan was getting in a tizzy about who was going to man the phones and send the patients in during surgery.'

'And you've stepped into the breach?' The solicitor sounded incredulous.

'I thought that I might pick up a little more evidence.'

'Ah,' said Mr McCormick. 'Now I believe you.'

Grace went back to the office and stood at the internal window, puzzling out the system. At the same time she was turning events over and over in her mind. Miss Dawburn had repeated in front of the nurse her boast that she had organised legacies for the doctor, so that made four witnesses to what amounted to a confession. That, together with the paper wrapping from the box of suppositories and whatever else the forensic scientists could discover, would surely solve the major problem. But was the dowager's secret intact? In her mind, she began to list everybody who knew or might know about the letters. She must get Mr McCormick to get Mr Hodges's brother to put pressure on his sibling to reveal the identity of his well spoken accomplice, and then to find some means of ensuring his silence. The solicitor seemed to be quite capable of manipulating people into doing whatever he deemed best for his clients, within the confines of his conscience.

It was surgery time. Between giving Doctor Broch a potted version of why she had replaced Miss Dawburn and sorting out the trickle of arriving patients, she soon decided that quite enough people were in a state of panic about the dowager's indiscretions. She, Grace, had more immediate things to worry about.

Four months had gone by. Miss Dawburn had made several court appearances and, while refusing to make any comments about the charges facing her, had used the occasions to proclaim her love for Dr Sullivan and to insist that the doctor was only waiting for the right moment to admit that it was reciprocated. A succession of legal representatives had been appointed but each had either resigned or been dismissed. The psychiatrists were still arguing over whether she was fit to plead.

There had been sufficient media publicity added to the local word of mouth to ensure that nobody any longer harboured any suspicions of Grace. The sole dissenting voice was that of Glenda Ashby, who had never forgiven Grace for her barbed retort; but Miss Ashby's spite was so widely known that her condemnation was all that was needed to confirm Grace's innocence.

Stuart continued to replace the photograph on the mantelpiece beside the urn. Grace stopped bothering to remove it except when visitors were expected. For her, it had become part of the scenery and so had lost its impact. Mrs Gillespie visited unexpectedly one day and studied the photograph for some seconds before remarking, 'I like your hair like that.' Grace was never able to decide whether her mother was showing a level of tact that had never previously revealed itself or had merely been astoundingly unobservant.

On a cold, clear day, Grace was looking out of the window and thinking of nothing in particular except that it was the season for root growth and the new garden would be gathering strength for its spring outburst. The winter had included several mild spells as a result of which the grass would soon need a cut, but Grace did not have to worry about that – free maintenance had been promised indefinitely. The snowdrops were up and forsythia was showing a single yellow flower. Snow was sparkling on the summit of Beinn Donuill. She turned away from the window and smiled. On the strength of Stuart's legacy from his uncle, the room had been transformed. The doctor, after learning how his patient had come to die, had refused to accept a legacy from such

a tainted source. Grace and Stuart had had no such scruples, so
there had been money in hand towards a second car.

The sound of the doorbell fetched her to the front door. She
glanced at her watch as she went but her first appointment with
a physiotherapy patient was not for an hour. She found a uni-
formed chauffeur, cap in hand. A large Mercedes with dark windows had arrived silently and was parked in the mouth of the
driveway. 'Mrs Campbell? Her Grace would be pleased if you
would join her in the car for a few minutes,' said the chauffeur.
'She asked me to explain that she does not walk as easily as she
once did.'

'Yes, of course,' Grace said. She managed a quick glance in the
hall mirror but her French roll looked reasonably tidy. Going for
a warm coat seemed inappropriate. She hurried through the cold
air. A rear door opened as she arrived. 'Get in, my dear,' said a
voice. 'Hodson, go for a walk.'

The chauffeur's uniform was smart but it did not look warm
enough for a walk on such a day. 'You can go into the house,'
Grace said.

The chauffeur was an elderly man, stooped from years of driving. He remained professionally impassive but smiled with his
eyes. 'Thank you, Ma'am.'

Grace ducked into the car. The chauffeur – Hodson – closed
the door with a gentle clunk. The dowager duchess was small.
Grace had the impression that she had shrunk with the years, but
her face was little lined and had once been beautiful. She wore a
lovely sable coat but the car was warm and the coat was open,
revealing what Grace thought was a rather ordinary twin-set. Her
rings were undoubtedly good. Her hair was white but full and
carefully dressed.

'So you're Stuart Campbell's wife.' The dowager's face was
animated but her smile brought wrinkles to her otherwise
smooth complexion. 'I never met your husband but his uncle
spoke of him so often that I feel that I know him. My letters
came back to me through your lawyer. I understand that you
found them and that it was your wish that they be returned to
me.'

Grace found her voice. 'That's so,' she said.

'And no thought of a reward, when it must have been obvious that the letters could have been turned into cash.'

'It wouldn't have been right, Your Grace.'

'Grace... I may call you Grace?' The dowager's voice was thin but she still had a warm laugh. 'And you had better call me Cecelia. We can't have two Graces in the car. My dear, you'll never know how much it meant to me to get my letters back. I'm very grateful. Not just because of the danger of scandal – Carradine and the others were wetting themselves in fear but I've lived far too long to worry about what people say.

'I've had a good life. Two good lives, really. There's been my public life. I think I've done some good – I hope so. And there's been a private life. Not many people in my position manage to have one. I've known love, real love, and I've managed to keep it out of the papers. Well, these things come to an end and those letters are all that are left of it. I can treasure them now while I make sure that nobody else gets to read them.'

'But that would be a shame,' Grace said. 'They're very moving and they're a piece of history. Could you not leave them in trust for, say, twenty years. By then, they won't hurt anybody.'

Her Grace smiled. Her eyes were looking into the far distance. 'It's an intriguing idea, but twenty years wouldn't be long enough. I have to think of my grandchildren. But I rather like to think of the world reading about my love, a hundred years from now. I'll have to think about it.' She brought her blue eyes back from the distance and looked into Grace's face. 'I've waited until now to express my gratitude, until I could be certain that nobody had talked. You must have seen the letters, so I don't have to convince you what a precious part of my life they represent. Do you truly love his nephew?'

'Very much so.'

'Yes, I see that you do. Then you'll understand. Is he good to you?'

'Always,' Grace said. 'When he remembers.'

'How typical!' The dowager laid a finger on Grace's hand. 'But I didn't mean is he kind to you. I meant, Grace, is he *good*? Is he strong? Is he a tiger?'

Grace hid a smile. 'He is,' she said, 'but only on those special occasions, the ones we're both thinking of. The rest of the time, he's sweet and gentle.'

The dowager sighed. 'How like his dear uncle!' (Grace wondered yet again if they could possibly be speaking of the same uncle.)

'And your son, Cecelia?' she asked.

'A chip off the old block, I think.' She did not say which old block and Grace dared not ask. From a pocket in the fur, the dowager produced a neat case. 'You haven't asked for a reward,' she said, 'but I would like to give you one anyway. I shall be deeply hurt if you refuse it. Most of my jewels are heirlooms but this is my own. My daughter-in-law already has more jewellery than she could lift. I'd rather that you had them than anyone else. I shall like to think of his nephew's wife wearing them.'

Grace opened the case. It held a modest necklace, a pair of earrings and a ring, all pearls and, she was sure, natural. But the jewels were not large enough to be ostentatious. A schoolmaster's wife could wear them in all modesty. Most observers would assume them to be cultured. 'Thank you so much,' she said.

'And you'll remember him?'

'I shall certainly do that,' Grace said with feeling. She tried not to think about the last occasion on which she had seen Stuart's uncle alive but it kept popping into her mind. 'I shan't forget him,' she said.

It seemed to be enough. The dowager nodded. 'And now I must go,' she said. 'I've done what I came for but I had to steal the time and it's a long road back to Balmoral.'

'Of course,' Grace said. 'Thank you again and goodbye.'

'Goodbye, my dear. Try to remember the poor old boy with kindness.' The dowager's voice broke on the last word.

The chauffeur must have been watching from the window because he came out as soon as Grace moved. She struggled for a minute with the heavy door, which gave him time to reach the car and open up for her. As she stood up, she was sure that he winked at her.

When the car had hissed softly away she hurried into the warmth, still puzzling over that wink. Surely chauffeurs to the nobility did not wink while on duty. She was still puzzling over it when she entered the sitting room and saw the photograph, shining brightly on the mantelpiece.